# THE TALES OF
# Harry Also

written and illustrated by
CELIA NORMAN SMITH

The Book Guild Ltd

First published in Great Britain in 2022 by
The Book Guild Ltd
Unit E2 Airfield Business Park,
Harrison Road, Market Harborough,
Leicestershire. LE16 7UL
Tel: 0116 2792299
www.bookguild.co.uk
Email: info@bookguild.co.uk
Twitter: @bookguild

Typeset in 11pt Minion Pro

Printed on FSC accredited paper
Printed and bound in Great Britain by 4edge Limited


ISBN 978 1915352 309


British Library Cataloguing in Publication Data.
A catalogue record for this book is available from the British Library.

*To Cooks*

"What he values is a task that demands all he has and all he is, absorbing him and therefore releasing him entirely."
*Nan Shepherd 'The Living Mountain'*

# Part One

# Spring

# Chapter One

At the foot of the Campsie Fells, between here and there, lies a beautiful garden. There are no pristine lawns of light and dark green stripes, or tidy herbaceous fissures, or contained ramblings on terraced Lovelace. There is little seen order in the margins except for the pruned east-west wisteria that puts lines onto this page. There are two conical spiral shrubs of box in sharp-scissor topiary at the steps to nowhere. Maybe you are nowhere, at least until you walk along the fine gravelled path to the vegetable garden. You glide on the crunch, crinch with every step and you float on that sound. A sweet drink of this organic air thrills you. You know not why but you're compelled to open the small metal latch and enter through the filigree whirls of an iron gate into this land that has the ability to envelop, charm and bombard all of your senses.

This is the vegetable garden for the large Pink House. You've guessed it, the house is painted pink, with grey windowsills and a big white welcoming door at the front. A crystal conservatory adorns one side facing south while at the rear door there is a lane to the farm. A small cottage (also pink) stands back from here, unassumingly clinging to a picket fence which contains a typical cottage garden of foxgloves, roses, herbs and an area marked as 'miscellaneous'. But it is the vegetable garden that holds the real delights, so let's explore it to see what we can find.

The air here is from the garden, of the garden, even though one sees very little to determine the scale of the place. Large cypress trees form a dark, blue-green tunnel with a delicate light at the end, enticing you inwards to a dreamland. Hold out your arms like a scarecrow and let your hands brush against these giant teardrop forms, so they can ooze their Mediterranean perfume. Walk onwards and there, suddenly: you are in the vegetable garden.

A bench of cherry wood, surrounded by a semi-circle

of herbs, lies recessed at the beginning of your journey. Come and sit a while, lean back on the pillows of thyme, rest your head next to the miniature rosemary forever fragrant and admire the neat, formal beds set out in traditional rotation. The vista is south, rising sharply to the dark horizon of the Campsie Fells: pink skies, rough skies, blue skies, all living skies, a picture framed. It is a great place to come with a cup of hot chocolate in hand, but beware, you may drift into that whispery state where dreams can envelop your mind and reality is lost.

Careful! Someone is pulling at your trouser leg!

"Excuse me! Have you seen Peawee? I need to ask him something really important."

A squiffy little voice, rising almost to a squeak, is determined to get your attention. It is Moleskin, a young underground dweller making a rare daylight visit to the upside world of the topside world of trees and sky. He sneezes out a plume of dust from his nostrils at the end of his little pink snout and then wipes his whiskers with his flat paws. He smells the air, not sure that he can trust his other senses. His eyes don't see well as they are small, almost entirely closed to keep out soil and flickerings of root tails; his ears are pinned back and his paws feel only to dig, parting the heavy soil, pushing soil out into the night.

His nose is his periscope to life beyond his self and up into the clean air. Sometimes, on days such as this, he has to come up in the daylight hours – a very rare occurrence, for only when he really needs to does a mole come aboveground. He prefers the fairly mundane existence of his tunnels, where he is safe. Above his homeland the world has a multitude of variants which cause him to panic and run away, wobbling from side to side with a whizzing heartbeat. Then he remembers to take a deep breath... and relax.

The soil is sweeter here, newly toiled, even warm. Thank goodness it wasn't raining.

Today, he needs to come upside, because today he must find Peawee the Wuidwisp, one of the tiny woodland fairy folk. The mole's little pink, whiskery nose twitches. He pants. Dewdrops of soil rustle in his fur as he levers himself out of his hole. He was very disappointed to find the garden deserted apart from Harry Also, a most handsome scarecrow, residing amongst the artichoke plants. Their soft, silvery leaves create the impression that Harry Also is sitting on a velvet-blue cushion. A long shadow, emanating from his legs, bumps along these sleepy plants, rising up over a huge, red brick wall on the north side of the garden – Harry Also could easily have been ten foot tall in the evening when shadows grow. His shadow mingles with the espalier trees of pears on the wall behind him. Their branches are full of blossom, warming in the sun with jewels on the pruned tips like ladies' fingers at a party, always attached to Harry Also but detached of the wall, hinged, disjointed with the illusion that he was sitting. Shadows cannot smile or chuckle. How can they even blink their eyes?

Harry Also is a fine chap, from his beautiful purple boots, to his earthy legs of hessian, to his dandy spotted scarf with large polka dots, to the top-most apple-pie bonnet on his straw curls. His large blue button eyes are all-seeing onto his patch of ground, because he has a job to do for a much bigger picture. Just for this moment a young mole needs his advice.

"I'm sorry, Moleskin, but Peawee is not here. He has gone away on one of his important travels. Can I help you? You seem most agitated."

This furry little creature beside Harry Also seemed to all the world as if someone had flattened him with an enormous boot. His little body was so close to the ground you couldn't see under him. No light came out the other side, so he couldn't even stamp his furry feet if he tried.

"But I want to know if spring has sprung," he insisted. "Peawee said he would alert me so that I can clear out my tunnels of the fusty winter mess that is down there. So much rubbish! It all builds up, you know. I want

Peawee. He's never around when I want him." Moleskin was getting very angry now and it didn't suit him.

Harry glared at Moleskin. "It isn't always what we want that is important, Moleskin, but what we need, and you don't need Peawee. You aren't thinking straight at the moment because Peawee is always helping others. He is the most caring of the woodland folk I know. Believe me, Moleskin, what Peawee is doing now is of great importance and he will return when he is good and ready. So you will have to do with me." Harry tried not to sound too angry himself, but he had attracted the attention of the little creature.

"*Craw-craw, craw-craw*." There was a rustle and a chuckle from above. A metallic-looking crow sitting on the scarecrow's shoulder opened one of his beady eyes to size up the situation.

"Well, Button-box, my old friend, we have a dilemma. Young Moleskin here needs to know if spring has sprung and he needs our help."

Button-box eyeballed the mole and decided the little furball was harmless. He would remember his face anyway.

"*Craw-craw*. Can he not tell by himself? I mean to say, let me see if I can explain more clearly." He took a deep breath to think a little. "The earth is warming up, perfect for worms, perfect for me – as I like to eat juicy worms – so warming-up time equals worming-up time. There!" One clear sentence in one big breath.

"I like eating worms too," remarked the mole, "but I

can't get at them if my tunnels are blocked up."

"Come now, Button-box, don't tease him so, for this is an important time of year. 'Spring is an impression of immortality', I once heard someone say."

"Oh yes, and what does that mean? You hear the strangest things from folk in this garden."

"It means that," emphasised Harry, "here in the garden, the trees fold away for winter, losing their pretty leaves and being dormant as if dead. Then we see those lovely pale green shoots in spring as they come back to life, eternal, they 'live forever', giving the impression of immortality."

"That is all very philosophical, but it doesn't answer my question," retorted Moleskin. This was all far too complicated for his little brain when it was in a muddle.

"Sorry, Moleskin, but they do say philosophers make good gardeners." Harry thought this very apt but Moleskin looked confused and a little irritated. "Perhaps we need to look closer to the ground, where the early signs of spring will be well on their way. There will be expressions of spring in the early flowers ready for an insect to pollinate them, to set their seeds for next year and the next generation. Ad infinitum, so to say," added Harry whimsically as he tried to give a more simple explanation, but seemed to be heading for trouble.

"Infa what?" asked the crow, quite bemused by this little show.

"It means going on forever. Ad infinitum," he repeated. "Interesting words, don't you think? Come on, Moleskin, you live in the dark lands – all you need is a little faith!" said Harry.

"Hey, and then you live forever!" exclaimed Button-box, very pleased with himself at the speed of his wit.

"Come now, Button-box, we must be serious now; it is a most important question that needs our full attention. Be a little more courteous and ponder the mole's dilemma. You are of the skies so when you fly around you can see to all the ends of the earth."

"Ad infinitum," butted in the crow.

"Yes, OK, Button-box, not bad!" Harry gave a chuckle. "As a crow you look for carrion to eat and then come back here, tummy full, to my cosy warm bonnet and have a nap. It all seems so simple to you. Moleskin needs to spring clean after a long winter. He moves unseeing, intimate with his dark environment looking for food. He smells every fibre, root or life underground so that he may eat and then sleep soundly. If he doesn't clean out his tunnels they will block up as quickly as a drainpipe full of autumn leaves. No nonsense now, let us make a list."

"What kind of list, Harry?" asked the mole, happy now that something constructive was happening.

"Pros and cons," said Harry, to the point.

"What are those? I need a simple 'yes' or 'no', not a list, for goodness' sake."

Moleskin was getting twitchy again.

"OK then, a simple 'yes' and 'no' list. They must be living encounters in time with no rules set down in writing. Let us be constructive in our observations. Who will go first?" Harry was now getting fully behind this unusual project, as Button-box jumped up and down. He had a clue.

"Your straw hands have not been thieved by the birds yet, so it isn't spring." The crow was very pleased with himself, but Harry soon brought him back down to earth.

"Very helpful, but birds can use all sorts of things to make their nests, and at different times in the year too."

"Like what?" chipped in Moleskin.

"Dry moss, sheep's wool, slumber soft goose down wafting up in the air where it is caught by the swallows. I have seen them swoop down, again and again, to pluck the tiny feather out off the breeze only to drop it and catch it up once more. That must be a fun game! I remember one year a pair of swallows made their nest in the stable block, above the tack-room door. They patiently constructed their nest by mixing up small gobs of mud and spitting them out onto the wall to form a cup under the eaves. It was so dry that year that the local radio asked folk to make large puddles of mud in their gardens, so the swallows and house martins could build their nests. The birds here lined their nest with moss and horsehair. Unfortunately, when their two fledglings tried to fly for the first time, the horsehair became their downfall, quite literally. As they tried to fly they plummeted to the ground, held tightly to each other by a binding of horsehair. A wing from each chick was so bound up with that of the other that together they looked like one bird with two heads. Fear took over and they huddled into the small, sunny corner of the building, barely breathing for fear of capture."

"Oh my goodness!" exclaimed Moleskin. "What happened next?" His eyes had filled with glassy tears.

"Cats got their tongues," beat Button-box. "*Craw-craw!* Cats got their tongues!"

"Don't listen to him, my furry friend, the cats did not get them and far from it. A happy coincidence occurred: Dolly the shepherd walked into the yard and noticed the situation. Her first thought was she had found an amazing biological phenomenon, but on closer inspection she was surprised to see the true predicament. She was able to gather them up and gently cut away the hair and release the two perfectly formed birds into the air. As they flew off a tiny blue feather, soft and sleek, sailed gently down to lie at her feet. She was sun-dazzled and put her hand up to shield her eyes, and she could see the young birds fly away, embracing life fully. She was dazzled too by the encounter, the closest of escapes and the good fortune that she'd been there, in that moment of time. There is a fine line between life and death, a hairline, which made her smile."

"Wow, they were two lucky birds. Is that a yes or a no to spring?" said Moleskin when Harry had finished his story.

"I think that is a no, as the swallows haven't arrived yet to start building their nests."

"Lovely story, though," said Button-box.

"Come on, Button-box, help us out. Who are the early birds nesting now?"

"Let me see," he said. "The sparrows have definitely started, as well as the blue tits in the penthouse bird box."

"Did you know, they call sparrows Spadgers in the West Country," mused Harry. "I just thought I would add that little gem of knowledge. Sorry, Button-box, carry on, I interrupted you."

"Yes, I saw Mrs Tom-tit gathering small twigs, moss and some tiny feathers. The male bird is very vocal with his *tee-tee-tee* call to all who have the time to stop and wonder at his call. He is an irascible fellow, full of mischief, darting about the trees with acrobatic precision. He is neat and tidy, but maybe not as handsome as I," topped the crow.

The others laughed with him.

"Sounds like spring is on its way, but we need to think nearer the ground for Moleskin's paws and his nose to feel if it has sprung," suggested Harry.

He knew he could see far beyond the mole's horizon. The scarecrow looked around too. Stop, look, what can you see? He remembered the game the children played. Or was it stop, listen, what do you hear? Both would do. So they did both.

"Look over there, guys, a really colourful coming of spring." Harry directed Moleskin to the narrow bed alongside the brick wall. Tiny, sharply blue groups of flowers, scillas mingled with grape hyacinths contrasting with the dashing yellows of tiny tête-à-tête daffodils. "My favourites are the primroses who have been flowering for ages this year. The cowslips in the fields are like tiny umbrellas of springtime. The crocuses are nearly finished and this year I had to be most vigilant, as the sparrows kept trying to eat all the flowers. What a mess they made before I managed to shoo them off." Moleskin was getting bored and had shuffled over to one of the freshly dug beds. It smelt so enticing, he could almost taste the sweetness. What was that at his paw tips? He pressed forward to investigate.

"Keep off!" shouted Harry. "No, oh my goodness, *no*! That is the garlic bed! If you break off their tiny shoots I will be in trouble!" But it was too late as Moleskin crushed a young plant, and the aroma drifted around them all.

"Oh, Harry, I am so very sorry," said the mole. "I didn't see the green shoot, but I sure could smell it. I think it is a little strong for my liking." His nose twitched with disapproval.

"Not to worry, it will grow another shoot as it is still a very young plant," replied Harry. "Look over there, the broad beans are well on their way up with lots of young leaves. I think we have enough signs for spring."

Moleskin was beginning to feel good about the list when Button-box chipped in.

"However!" he said, and there was a long pause.

"Oh dear, now what?" asked the mole, losing all his new-found joy.

"There was a frost last night, so maybe it is still winter

here." The crow was trying to keep the suspense going as an encore to this amazing debate; he could keep it going for ever. "It even snowed two days ago and the bird bath had sparkles all across the surface. There is no way the soil will be warm enough to plant potatoes. Then, of course, we can't forget—"

"I once heard a story," interrupted Harry. The crow looked at the ground, defeated.

"Another of your fine stories, Harry. Where do you get them from? I mean, you can't exactly go anywhere, stuck to your pole," asked the mole, still twitching.

"No, I can't, but the stories can come to me. Lots of folk come to visit these gardens and they love to stop a while at this bench and natter. Of course, I can hear all their woes and heartaches as well as some wonderous and funny stories. Like the time a farmer told of his method of knowing when the soil was warm enough to plant his potatoes."

"And when would that be?" asked the mole.

"When he could bare his cheek to the soil," replied Harry.

"Oh no!" piped up Button-box with a wry smile. "But which cheek did he mean? It could be a sight for sore eyes!"

They all burst out laughing. Moleskin was more relaxed now amongst his new friends but added that he was still seeking the definite clue that he knew Peawee would use to answer his question.

Harry stared into nothing. "Remember, we all

see things differently, so most will certainly see signs in different ways. Everything is somehow connected to everything else. However small or irrelevant that connection may seem, we can still translate those sets of circumstances and find your answer, Moleskin."

# Chapter Two

Harry seemed to have drifted in and out of his mind with images and connections of his garden, his domain. He was consumed by the moment. You could make any number of lists, but if you're not careful spring would quite simply pass you by, while you spend a lifetime in search of these happenings to experience the essence of spring.

Just look around, turn over a stone and enjoy nature's environments, wherever you are. Much of what he sees, tastes or delights in will be there long after his trousers have faded and the straw all plucked out from his body, like the early orange-tip butterfly and the other early-emerging brimstone. These are two regular early springtime invaders of the meadows, flitting here and there low over the grass sward looking for a mate 'The Heralds of Spring'.

There is an essence to the seasons, of that he was sure, but it can't be bottled or preserved in gin. He remembered why Dolly is always happy this time of year, filled with new life. Lambing time. That is why she had been anxious and jittery for a few weeks now, but it is her favourite time of the year, however tired or cold she gets.

"Of course!" he shouted. Harry was back! "Of course! It is lambing time. Go to the field, just there next to the apple trees. On the other side of the fence are two lambs who were born a couple of days ago."

Button-box needed no invitation and immediately flew over to see if there was some afterbirth for him to nibble on, but it was long gone, so he waited for the mole to make his way to the fence between garden and field. Their movement drew the attention of one old ewe who stood and stretched, her two lambs stirring by her side. The lambs were pure black with a little white star on top of their curly foreheads, one lamb quite little and the other a bit bigger.

"Hallo, lambs, how are we today? What did they name you two?" asked Harry.

"They have been called Little Bit and Big Bit," charmed the ewe, obviously content with her beautiful offspring.

The lambs immediately tried to find their mother's teats for the taste of the intensely warm milk. Her udder was not easy to find under the thick woolly fleece, but they managed and gave a contented shiver that went all the way through their curly fleeced bodies to the very end of their wagging tails. Wiggle, wiggle, wiggle.

"I see more new lambs out in the field," said Button-box, and flew over to investigate. Suddenly he was behaving a little crazed, jumping up and down, talking to the mother of the new lambs.

"What are they talking about?" asked Moleskin.

"I don't know," said Harry, "but Button-box is having a fit of laughter. I wonder what has tickled his wings." He waved his arms. "Is everything all right with the lambs?"

Button-box finished his crazed dance and flew back to his pals. "*Craw-craw!*" He giggled. "The old ewe has had triplets and guess what Mrs D from the Pink House has called them? You will never guess." The crow could barely finish his sentence and almost fell off Harry's bonnet. "She's had one ram lamb and two tiny ewe lambs, and their names are…" Poor Button-box had to pause to regain control; he was finding it hard to even speak now, he was chuckling so much.

"Well?" demanded Harry.

"Well," continued the crow, "she has called them Stew and the Driblets!" And he was off again, giggling like popping corn.

Moleskin looked at Harry and Harry tried to look at Button-box, but he had fallen off his perch in a fit of laughter.

"I don't get it, what is so funny?" asked Moleskin, bemused with all this commotion over a silly name.

"It's like this, young mole," said Harry. "Stew is a boy's name, or a casserole dish with meat and vegetables in it. Driblets is a play on two words: one is to dribble, as in down your chin, and the other is giblets, as in the inners of a chicken, used to make a thick gravy."

"But the funniest thing is the name sounds like a Motown pop group from the swinging '60s," added Button-box. "They once called a couple of lambs Sonny and Cher because they had long tails, and last year there was a huge single lamb born and they named him Iron Lamb."

All the commotion had set into motion a strange happening amongst the lambs. Content on their milk feed, they charged off down the fence line. At the corner post they suddenly stopped, turned and charged all the way back. They repeated this several times, then began to gambol in one unified motion and spring straight up into the air, lifting off the ground from all four feet in one coordinated prance. Boing, boing, boing.

"There!" announced Harry triumphantly. "Look, Moleskin, spring has sprung!"

Harry drifted free from his yes-or-no list. He now understood why Peawee was so good at answering the tiny mole's question: he just observed many things in time and space. Harry let go his mind, let go the burden of the knowing, and cheerfully told the mole to clear out his tunnels. There was no specific date, just an overwhelming blanket of feelings combining on the breeze, like gossamer over the meadow. But if acknowledgement was needed, what better way than these lambs who, blossom by blossom, take large leaps forward in a quest for their spring.

He contemplated all about him at this time of year; he was never too old to learn something new or feel new emotions. That's what scarecrows do. He thought of Peawee gone away on a journey and hoped his friend would find his answers too. He hoped he was safe. Like floodwater collecting stones as it whooshes downstream, all the knowing we collect along our way erodes our being and our thoughts until we are mature and sculpted. Different ways beguile different valleys, but it is the journey down that valley that will triumph, gathering strength along its path.

The garden is here every year, all year, and it is the garden that grows with the knowing. One cannot know a garden unless it is seen from a beginning, however rough, unkempt or even manicured. Return to it time and again, enjoy it as a visitor, break into the circle dance or leave at any time and you will be a better person for it. That is what gardens can do. Ask yourself: is the garden better for your intrusion?

Harry had thought hard about these situations many times and each year he did his best to help the garden grow. He was sure PC the Pussy Cat was better at scaring things away. If a rabbit dared to venture under the fence, looking for a tasty morsel, it may get away with a lettuce lunch on one occasion, but the same small animal would never see another day if it tried a second time. If a rabbit was caught there would be nothing left of it except an empty skin of muffled fur, its feet and its stomach – PC would see to that. Harry could always hear the crunch of the bones and it made his straw shiver up and down his spine. Come to think of it, he hadn't seen PC about recently. She'd been heavily pregnant last time she'd been in the garden, so maybe another small life was opening its eyes on this world.

Harry was brought back from his dream state by the mole tugging again at his trouser leg. "Are you in a trance, Harry, or had you nodded off? I can't tell as your eyes seem wide open even though you are not seeing or hearing us. Harry, are you there?"

Harry didn't like being pulled back from his dream state. He lost all momentum of thought. Maybe he was growing old.

"A mixture of the two," Harry said at last. "I can't always tell which myself."

The answer seemed to satisfy Moleskin. Harry was drifting; it had been a long day for the scarecrow so the mole decided not to demand any more of him today. Instead he muzzled up to Harry, wiping his scent up and down the trousers with a show of endearment.

"Thank you, Harry. I appreciate your time and those stories we love to hear, but I must be on my way. Got to go, got to shuffle the rubbish from my door. Beware the dust cloud!" With that Moleskin sneezed, rubbed his pink eyes and was gone, off to find his mole hill.

"Well, Button-box, my dear friend," said Harry, "I

think we've had an enhancing day. Could you do me one last favour?"

"Anything, Harry," sighed the crow.

"Could you scratch between my shoulder blades? I have such an infernal itch in my straw."

"Of course, Harry," said Button-box. He moved on down the shoulder and, leaning over as far as he dared without falling off, he dug his beak into the wadded mass of straw.

"Up a bit, ooh! Now left a bit. That feels so good."

"Just a little bit or a big bit?" asked the crow.

"Where would we be without your sense of humour, my friend? Thank you, thank you."

The sun was setting on the garden. The crow finished his task, groomed himself and promptly tucked his head under his wing and began to snore. Shadows of deep midnight blue hung around the fringes and soon the moon would mingle amongst the stars. Harry could feel the chill across his face and the drifting feeling returned. Maybe Dolly would come to check the sheep late into the night. There was one Shetland ewe still to lamb and she had started the routine pawing at the ground in one corner of the field, which was a good sign of an imminent birth. Harry had never seen a live birth before; he had always fallen asleep or dark clouds had prevented a good view. Tonight, however, was a full moon. Tonight's the night. He must stay awake; this far north daylight is languid. Soon the land would merge with the stars.

# Chapter Three

Harry was dragged back to reality by the crackling of a bonfire. How long did he sleep for? Did he miss the birth again? What was going on at this time of night? Over by the compost bins lay a large pile of winter prunings and Dolly had come out into the night to start a bonfire. Not only would it keep her warm and get another little job done, but the air around a fire crackles with life, jumps about in the air and drags you inwards to its heat and power. Harry was very glad the compost was away on the other side of the garden near the henhouse. Sparks and straw do not go together well!

The bonfire sparkled up into the night air to mingle with the stars. With the full moon all movement around him intensified. Alert now, he could make out the girl's small figure enveloped in a huge sheep skin jacket. She looked toasty warm. She had two companions with her. There was Chai, the old collie bitch who was deaf and half blind, tenacious and true, plus the young dog Bobby, all bounce but a hard worker once he was on the job. Both dogs were superb at lambing time. They were gentle around the lambs, never questioning a command and the greatest of companions during a long night. For them too there was nothing better than to sleep under the stars, waiting for the embers to fade as morning approaches.

Dolly had made time to come and await the final birthing. She didn't need to stay; she just wanted an excuse to do so, to dwell here and feel the chilled air. She lay down alongside the compact fire and the dogs cuddled into her back. There was a closeness to the earth as her features glowed in the firelight, the bonfire, charcoal and was that the dew already? She rolled over to stare up at the morning star, Venus the planet, Venus the Roman goddess, Venus the expression of love and desire.

Harry knew his desires; he had no occupation but to sleep, empty his mind. He just… wan… ted… to… see… a… *birth… Stay awake, Harry!*

He needed this attention to detail, to learn more about the nature beyond his garden. Just over the fence was this very opportunity. Maybe his longing would dilute the reward – was he expecting too much from this? There was a comet in the north-west. Low in the sky it blazed its two tails, one of fluorescent blue and the other a large silver trail. It faded and rekindled back into life so brightly that the girl shrieked like a small weasel at play. Clear frosty nights were over for this year, but Hale-Bopp would blaze on for a few more months.

Harry could hear in the stillness the clear call of a tawny owl. He was keeping his senses together, his spine to tingle, his eyes to see, his ears to hear, his thoughts to be. Silhouetted against the coming of the day were three owls flying past low along the fence line. Large flapping movements propelled them on their wings, drifting past Harry almost unnoticed. They called a preliminary short *oo-oo*. It was repeated in a long, quavering and beautiful manner, *oo-oo-oo-oo*. It is the music of the woodland night, warm colours of a song. The tawny owls made a hole through the air and Harry captured their essence. Harry engaged now with the dawn. The mystery of consciousness is akin to an artist stripping back her sketchbook, to allow her expressions to surface for her to replicate them in stone, paint, wood or clay.

Awake! Did he miss the birth? Was that the morning over the Campsies, the hills to the south? Was the dawn here already? There was an urgency in the dewy mist, a sound of giving, a slip of the waters, a catch of breath; life was on its way.

Harry could see the ewe panting. He was wide awake now. The dogs sat up and the girl moved silently away from the ashes to be nearer the ewe. She spoke softly to the old sheep, who responded with a deep baa. There was a bond between the shepherd and her flock. She walked the fields each day talking to them, telling them her woes and delights. Now at lambing time they trusted her voice and let her approach. Harry heard a farmer say that the best fertiliser for your fields was your boots. The girl's thick jacket hid another surprise, for she too was pregnant. It would be her second child. Harry heard a shout.

"Mummy! Has she had her lamb yet? Can I come into the field and see it?" A little girl no more than five was leaning through the fence. She was wrapped up tight, with an eider down over her shoulders and her baggy pyjamas sticking out at the bottom into her red wellies. Her mum had texted back to the cottage to join her and her dada had brought her down to the field, and now he lifted her over the fence without losing her wellie boots and placed her safely down next to Dolly. He chatted a while before returning back to the pink cottage not far away.

"Come closer, little Rose." Quietly the mum helped her young daughter to be beside her. All was prepared for this moment with a bale of straw nearby to sit on and the two girls sat huddled together, a warm bond on a chilly dawn with misty breaths rising. The ewe's panting intensified. No words were spoken, the mother and child simply hugged, watched and waited. The mood changed when the ewe lay down on one side and with each contraction she gave a hefty push. Her head strained backwards, her front feet digging into the earth as the birthing canal dilated, revealing the damp, pale shape of two tiny front hoofs. Another push and a small black nose rested on the forelegs. The opening was pure pinkness and the waters lubricated the lamb out. It entered this world in one determined, floppy, wet puddle of birth. It lay there, just lay there, like a stranded jellyfish on a sandy beach, helpless, lifeless.

The ewe stood up, turned to face her lamb and started to lick the birthing fluid away. She must lick the membrane away from the lamb's nostrils and mouth or it will die, suffocated in the very life-support bubble it grew in. The lamb was now eager to live; instinct and desperation in even quantities forced this lamb into action. It flailed its head from side to side, freeing the wet, mucus gunge from its face. It must take a breath now; it only has one chance. It forced out a tiny pant, enabling it to draw in that breath. Was it enough? The dark small tongue was hungry to feed on life, but would it taste life? The ewe continued to lick away the remains of the birth, encouraging her lamb with sounds, sweet mumblings, with her tongue moving over her lips from side to side, forming this guttural, gentle baa, the sound made only for a newborn. As she cleaned her lamb so she tasted her lamb's uniqueness, and when it was dry she would accept only that taste, that lamb. It had survived and would soon find its feet and its mother's teat for the first warm, thick, custard-like colostrum milk. It would guzzle it up and be content.

The little girl put her hand gently on her mother's swollen belly and looked up into her eyes, speaking in a near whisper: "Are you going to have a little lamb, Mummy?"

# Part Two

# Summer

# Chapter Four

Can scarecrows cry? Button-box was sure he had seen Harry's cheeks wet with tears that early dawn day, when they had witnessed a lamb being born, a tiny life flipflopping into the chilled morn. It had been a few weeks now and Harry had drifted into a parallel universe.

A new emotion had taken over his body. A measure of this new state seemed to be a capacity to overwhelm him at any time of the day or night. At the dawn of a new day he would be dilatory in his waking; he did not want back. He knew another dimension existed, perhaps between waking and sleeping, or out there amongst the stars. This surely wasn't all there is? The children from the Pink House came to the garden with their games of aliens and rockets from the skies. Other planets are out there in the darkness, with life, of that he had no doubt. Somewhere out there, he thought as he looked up.

There was much to enchant him in this garden, so why look to the stars? Look at the trees, for example, the silver birch with leaves that cover the tree like a green mist, tiny oval shapes, all glassy and delicate. The lime trees, bursting with fresh new colour all down the avenue to the Pink House. And the white beams' buds, visible all winter, that suddenly explode forth their young leaves covered in a thick coating of woolly down – they open as if sprinkled in flour and when the wind blows they shimmer all silvery and new. The very old yew tree on the way to the vegetable garden, standing as wide as it is tall, permanently green with a fine floor of ancient, discarded leaves – people run here for shelter when a sudden storm opens the heavens with a downpour of heavy rains. It is always the trees that people remarked upon, more alive, more significant, more real.

The visitors were sure to start coming soon to the garden now that summer was on its way. The swifts were screaming in the skies, the swallows *ticking-ticking* to each other, all heralding the new season and happy to be back after their long, very long, migratory flight. There was no mistaking the sound of the cuckoo from the woods where the very warmth and balmy surroundings acted like a sound box, vibrating it outward. Yet some folk come and never see what is there at their feet, or touch what can be touched or smelt. Are they the same in their worlds? Some ask questions and hear the answer, but they will never truly listen.

Harry was always happy to have visitors. They came to admire the garden and sat a while talking to each other, unaware that he was hearing their tales, some wondrous, some sad. He had the capacity and patience to soak these up. Perhaps it was a measure of a new thing in a story that he could then relate to his friends and creatures around him. His only way out of this garden was by these stories.

Today was a working day and he could feel the sun on his face, delicious to the very end of his pointy, carrot-like nose! It twitched with excitement for the new day and what it may bring. He felt renewed, like a bubbling source of water high up in the hills of the Campsies. He had been hiding his emotions from himself up to that very defining moment when the lamb was born and quivered under the pressure, but shook the cobwebs from under his bonnet. Button-box was unnerved by this sudden movement and flew off towards the orchard.

It was early in the day and he had to pull himself

together. He could hear approaching footsteps on the gravel that sounded delicate, not rough, tiny pit-a-pats, and Harry was suddenly wide awake to the sounds. It was PC, the Pussy Cat, a stunningly beautiful black cat with four white socks, chest and muzzle. She had entered the garden accompanied by another smaller cat, her kitten. She gracefully leapt over the fence and then waited for her kitten to climb up the wooden fencepost and lumber backwards down the other side. The kitten was understandably nervous, but PC was always looking back to encourage her offspring.

"Well, good morning, PC, and what do I spy with you this fine morning? We haven't seen you for a week or so, but now I can see why. Come close, little one, let us see you." Harry tried to ease the kitten forward with little endearments and sweet noises. With eyes popping and legs all a-wobble the little white bundle of furry nerves gingerly approached and looked up at Harry.

"My name is Lucy, so I am told," meowed the kitten. "Everything around me is so humungous, I can't seem to focus on one thing at a time. There is so much to see and do!"

"Hallo, Lucy, and welcome to the vegetable garden. It is good to meet you – you are a pretty wee thing. Is this your first adventure?" Harry knew very well that it must be; he simply wanted to relax the little kitten. "And congratulations, PC," he added.

PC launched herself up onto the cherry bench and was stretching out to warm every centimetre of her tummy. She had been cooped up in the stable loft for some time, only coming out at night to drink or catch a mouse or two, or three. Now this was heaven, on a bench in the sun.

"Meeeeeeeeeeeeow."

"Is this your first time in the garden?" asked the kitten.

"Oh no," replied Harry. "I have been here quite some years now."

"Were you born in the stable loft too?" the kitten continued. She hardly seemed afraid of anything just now, although her mother was on the lookout for trouble. Maybe BbC was about. The Big black Cat was a fine fellow but could get just a little enthusiastic for his size.

"No, Lucy, I was put together here in the garden. In fact, it was about this time of year I arrived after poor Old Harry decided he couldn't stand anymore. The first thing I remember was the sweetest scent; it filled my world as I was transported along, tucked under a large man's arm. There were children everywhere with cries of jollification, giggles and screams of delight. A huge bunch of pheasant-eye narcissus was being carried along with me and it was from these flowers that the overwhelming fragrance came. These small, unpretentious blooms had the most delicate white petals; they sweep backwards from the stem and are curved along the edges, but the name comes from the centrepiece. Here the three pollen-laden stamens are held inside a tiny, lime-green trumpet of which the edge is a bright orange fringe. They flower long after the large, pompous yellow daffodils are over and are a wondrous presence in the fields. An old lady, who sat on this bench, once recalled how her mother used to send her a box of these meadow flowers – it was in the 1950s when she was first married and a long way from home, and they came all the way from Switzerland to remind her of her mountain homeland. Isn't that a lovely thought?"

Harry rambled on a little, but Lucy seemed not to mind. In fact, she was engrossed.

"Who put you together?" asked Lucy, while playing with his trouser leg.

"It was Jake, the gardener. Of course, all the children were here, and Mrs D had brought homemade ginger beer for them and half a bottle of champagne."

"What is champagne?"

So many questions from a little cat, thought Harry.

"It is adult lemonade," said Harry, quick to think of something, as he wasn't quite sure himself of the answer.

"What happened next?"

"Jake took a large wooden mallet and knocked my pole into the ground, then he attached my head firmly on top. I could now see the magic of the world before me. Wow, I thought, wow and wow again! My head was spinning, literally as they twisted it onto the pole, then one nail and it was secure."

"Wow-meow!" said Lucy.

"Mrs D then put my fine scarf around my neck. A little girl put a bunch of droopy bluebells in my hand and I was complete."

"But who gave you your name?" mused the kitten.

"It was another of the little girls who asked what my name was and Mrs D told her it was Harry. Then a boy, who seemed to be taking no notice of the proceedings as he played with his toy truck in the gravel, looked up and asked: 'Harry also?' 'Of course!' Mrs D exclaimed. 'Harry Also!' You see, Lucy, the last scarecrow had been named Harry, so it was very clever of the boy to remember this, and that was how I came to be Harry Also, scarecrow of this vegetable patch. They all cheered as they gathered close to me and put their arms around me, everybody did in one ginormous 'Granny hug', as they called it. It felt so good to be in the garden."

On to the next thing, as Lucy chased a fly. She ended up at the greenhouses and started to play with her reflection in the glass. There were still a few trays of young seedlings on the benches, but most of these plants were now either in the cold frames hardening off or planted out in neat rows in their beds. The large greenhouse was now filling up with tomatoes, melons and early lettuce, and someone was even trying to grow tobacco! There were no cold winds this year, so these small gems of plants were growing away faster than Harry had ever seen before. There would be a glorious bank of colour later on for all to see.

There was so much going on. A sudden noise interrupted the group and PC sprang to life. She grabbed Lucy by the thick scruff on her neck and hurried away with her kitten swaying awkwardly in her mother's jaws. This powerful jaw gripped Lucy so tightly that PC was able to bound off, leap up and over the fence and away to the safety of a nearby thicket in no time at all. But who had disturbed them and what was all that noise?

It was feeding time for the sheep. Of course, each morning Dolly would appear with the bright yellow feed sack and sprinkle the dry mix onto the grass as she walked along, smartly followed by the very noisy ewes. She would call, "Come on," which seemed almost unnecessary but added to the drama. Heads in, tails up and lambs bouncing everywhere. Happy times, feeding times.

# Chapter Five

"*Craw-craw, craw-craw!*"

Button-box appeared on the scarecrow's shoulder. He was silky and new with colour as the sun reflected his jet-black feathers to a shiny lacquer. Black as jet, black as Jessop and black as the new moon. However, he is of the 'Yellow-Spot' tribe, which means that somewhere on his crow-black body is a yellow spot – his yellow spot is on his back directly between his wings. His brother has a yellow tail feather, while his father had a majestic yellow spot on his forehead resembling a small crest and his mother a few tiny yellow feathers around her left eye. Button-box seemed somewhat agitated and he could not contain his excitement.

"*Craw-craw, craw-craw!* I've seen Peawee, I've seen Peawee!" he shouted.

Harry looked up at his friend. "Thank goodness for that," he said, "I was getting just a little concerned for him, to tell the truth."

Button-box and Peawee were his greatest friends, like his children some would say. He always worried about them when they were away. Not everyone liked crows and some of their habits can be offensive in certain people's minds, but the 'Yellow Spot' tribe was dear to Harry.

"Where did you see him and how did he seem?" Harry was very concerned for his friend.

Peawee is a small, slim fellow of the Wuidwisps, a whisper in the treetops. He is the same size as the tree fairies, but the Wuidwisps have no wings, only amazing hands and feet on the end of spindly limbs that move like the wind to climb any tree before them. Even their hair is a streamlined spiral, spinning upwards to a fine point on top. They are swifter than the red squirrels that dwell there and leave magical trails, like gossamers in the air, as they move swiftly amongst the branches. It only lasts a small second and the trail is gone, but if the breeze catches one of these threads it will chime sweetly.

It is the skin on their feet and hands that hides their mystical magic; they are covered in little scales that grip the bark and other surfaces. You can't see the scales, for they lie flat in the palm of the hand, until the Wuidwisp lands on a tree and grips it. The tiny scales are forced open and they are secure. Imagine, the Wuidwisp is locked on as strongly as teasel seeds stick on a woolly sheep. Then, as they leap off, the scales swiftly retract. Some of the tree fairies have similar scales on their hands, but nothing akin to the Wuidwisps, who can move like lightning and jump like acrobats. There is no woodland they cannot master; the forests are their dimension. They build their homes in the fissures of the bark, the deep holes and recesses in the old oaks, beech and chestnut, and here also in the old yew tree.

Not only are they tiny and quick; they are also difficult to see with their camouflage. Some would say they are dull and musty, but their attire is a microcosm of shapes and shadows. The tree canopy is a wonderland playground for them with delights that we shall never know; like the owls they are all-seeing yet rarely seen. For the people who encounter these delicate folk it is a joy, but they know not to speak of their sightings, or these rare wisps may be lost forever to the punishments and miseries that man can inflict.

"*Craw-craw, craw-craw!* Are you there, Harry? Are you there, Harry Also?" The crow sounded confused, because he couldn't tell what Harry was thinking now his eyes were towards the woods, longing to see Peawee. Harry seemed overly worried – why would Harry be so concerned? Peawee looked after himself, a jolly enough fellow under all that hair, always with a tune in his heart. He played for all who wanted a tune, with a small dock-stem whistle which he kept hidden in a special pocket sewn into the shoulder of his jacket, like a bowman's quiver for his arrows. Wherever Peawee landed, the trees' leaves around him became wistful hearts. He cared for so many others, he gave the presence of not needing help himself. So why was Harry so concerned?

"Is there something you are not telling me about our friend, Harry? You have been a very quiet, contemplative fellow since Peawee went away a couple of months ago." Button-box settled down now and tucked his wings in, leaning his head down on one side to look into Harry's eyes. He had such sharp vision, none better than he at seeing through a subtle disguise; maybe he could even see around corners! "Come on, Harry! Where did Peawee go that is so mystifying and why do you care anyways?"

Harry decided he had to tell his friend and now was a good time. "Peawee went away to care for his terminally ill foster mother, and he stayed with her to the end. I have been very worried about him because she died a while back and I have not heard from him or his folk. No-one can say how they will be affected by such a loss. Maybe I shouldn't be so concerned."

"You are just a big softy, Harry, and I love you." There. Button-box had said it; it seemed the right time to tell his old friend these words. He wasn't always the joker in the pack.

"I wish I could tell you what is in my heart, Button-box," mumbled Harry.

"Do scarecrows have a heart in all that straw?" replied the crow.

Poor Harry didn't understand – was that a rhetorical question? There was no mechanical pumping organ inside his straw chest, but he strongly cared about life and the garden around him. All he had were his stories to tell. He wanted to be as a pebble thrown into still waters; he wanted the ripples he made to gently spread across his world and beyond to touch others. There was a responsibility to escape beyond his boundaries. However, his responsibility to Peawee was almost paternal; his very insides ached and he didn't like how he felt. Somehow the crow knew he wouldn't get an answer to his rhetorical question and felt stupid now that he had even asked it of his friend.

"You have a bond with Peawee," he said. "It is a deeper understanding than most other people and because of it you are all churned up inside. To have lost his foster mother, so dear to him, will leave him empty and lost." Button-box was beginning to understand why his friend had been so distant. "I'll go and find Peawee – he is close by, I am sure. I'll say you want to see him." He flew off before Harry could even blink.

Harry watched the bird fly south, up and across the fields towards Handbag Wood. Whenever the honeybees swarmed from the home hives, they would follow the same track from the orchard up to the apiary in Handbag Wood, to take up residence in another hive set to catch these swarms. It brought a smile to Harry's face, as the bees always gave mischief.

"No-one can tell bees what to do," said Harry out loud.

"A bit like Peawee!" replied PC, who had returned after all the commotion of feeding time had died down.

"Can crows get stung by the bees?" asked a small meow of a voice. It was Lucy, once more clawing at Harry's trousers.

"No, I don't think birds can get stung by bees, little Lucy, but humans have to put a special suit and veil on as they have to protect their thin skin. I remember one hot summer's day Mrs D and Dolly came through the garden all smartly dressed in their chalk-white bee suits, pushing a large wheelbarrow full of tools to work on the hives. You can just see the two home hives over there in the orchard. Dolly was giggling when she said they were off to '*Cherchez la femme*'. Apparently this means, in French, they were off to find the lady."

"What lady?" asked Lucy. "I didn't know they have lady bees."

"There are thousands of bees in a hive, and all the workers are female but only one can lay eggs, and she is called the queen bee. So the 'lady' they were off to find was the queen bee, so they could make sure she was well and laying lots of eggs, and then give her a dot of colour on her back to mark her. This would make it easier to find her next time. There may even be a little early honey for tea." Harry raised his eyebrows towards the orchard. "I could see them in the orchard from here. They lit some paper and small pieces of old hessian rags in this tin-can contraption, which has a funnel on top and a small set of bellows at the side. Dolly worked the bellows and out came a continuous plume of thick smoke. They approached the entrance of one of the Wormit hives and gave ten puffs of the smoker into it."

"What does that do? Apart from make all the bees cough!" said Lucy.

"It cons the bees into believing there is a fire nearby and they think they may have to leave their home, so they fill their guts with honey just in case of this emergency. While they are busy doing that the ladies can open the hive and work the bees without getting stung too many times. They don't want the bees to die, you see. Each sting has a barb on it, which the bee pushes into the skin, and when the bee flies off the sting remains, but unfortunately it rips the gut out of the bee's body too and it dies."

"Wow!" gulped Lucy. "That's not fair – when I protect myself I use my claws but I don't die when I scratch something. Poor things."

"It does seem strange. Maybe that is why they only sting when they really have to." Harry wished he knew the answer to this question of why some insects sting and don't die, while the lovely honeybee has to die.

He continued his tale before Lucy got bored. "It was a lovely, hot sunny day and most of the bees were out foraging for pollen and nectar. Once the roof was off and the top honey super – that's the box of frames – laid to one side, they could start to take out each individual brood frame. Somewhere on these beautiful hexagonal combs was the queen bee. It was a painstaking job as their eyes strained to look amongst so many bees, but she has a slightly larger abdomen then her female workers and this is for laying her eggs, one egg in every tiny cell." Harry was marvelling in this mystery of the beehive and the social network contained within, where every bee somehow knows what its job is. How and why was the question he had never heard an explanation for, but to be part of one group such as the honeybees' social network was mind-boggling. Did they have a map of the hive or the world outside? Did they argue? He only knew what the ladies talked about on their way to the hives.

"Then what, did they find the queen bee?" Lucy directed Harry's thoughts back to his story and he continued.

"The mass of worker bees running to reach the safety of the darkest shadows made the ladies' heads spin. The hives are happy hives and slowly the ladies cleaned each frame, inspecting them as they went, before they put them back into the hive. Still no queen. Eventually, on one of the lower brood frames, there she was! The large queen bee surrounded by young worker bees, like petals on a daisy forming a rosette, as they groom and feed her.

They quiver their bodies and dance to the music of her scent. It is an aroma alive with passion and needs to which she must be adored; if they fail her she will die. She is unable to feed herself the pure 'royal jelly' that creates and sustains her. All summer long she will lay thousands of eggs and the hive can swell to fifty thousand or more bees. So they found and marked the queen with a bright-coloured dot on her back, a good job done, so they closed up the hive."

"Wow again," said Lucy, and then she was gone, up and away over the fence to look for the hives. PC followed her slowly, to keep a motherly eye on things.

Harry loved all this activity at the hives. He would watch the bees on the flowers of the peas, the bumblebees on the broad beans and later at the end of July the lime trees would be humming – literally buzzing – with a cacophony of thousands upon thousands of insects' wings in a giant frenzy for the rich nectar. It makes one of the finest honeys in the world. One of the best imaginings too!

# Chapter Six

The day was moving on. Jake was busy watering the plants in the greenhouses and in the large plastic tunnel containing the carrots and very early potatoes. He had been harvesting these super-sweet early vegetables as well as the salads from the tunnel, long before the outside ones were ready. That's the beauty of these tunnels. Harry always looked at the hand baskets full of these gems of delight and wondered how they might taste; they looked so sweet and clear-skinned, and the children would just sink their teeth into the carrots with squeals of yumminess.

He recalled a day when one of the children had

squeezed a small ripe tomato in her hand with the seeds and their pulp oozing from her hand.

"Why did you do that?" Jake asked, looking a bit bemused. "It is a waste now, as we can't eat it."

"I just wanted to see how it felt to be a tomato," replied the little girl, promptly popping the whole thing in her mouth, "and I haven't wasted it 'cause it is *yummy*!"

Jake could only try to hide a laugh at this cheeky reply but failed; maybe she did feel how it was to be a tomato. The child's face was now full of sweet, sticky pulp and seeds, red like a clown's nose, so how could he be cross? "That's OK, little one," he said, "but only this once."

Harry longed for the taste of tomatoes, honey and the crisp vegetables to come to him, and later on in the summer it would be harvest time just right for his imaginings.

It helped that he had the best imagination in the world. But for now he was not imagining Peawee. Peawee was close by; Harry could sense him. Peawee was capable of absorbing all around him and releasing it completely in a split second. He had gravitated to the ground at Harry's feet, bringing the taste, the very essence of the forest floor, with him. He held a handful of this depth up to Harry.

"She's gone, Harry, my foster mother has died and she is at peace."

Before Harry could think of something to say Peawee had started to sing. Harry thought it a lullaby because the voice was softness, pure and simple. The words told of a time of the passing from one dimension into another, into the shades of sleep, a deep sleep.

"If I grow old with you, give me time.
If I don't remember you, don't cry.
If I stand and stare remember I am there,
For I am forever in your heart.

"My spirit may be weary, show me your smile.
My dreams may surrender, let me sleep awhile.
Our laughter can be heard for we will dance again,
As I am forever in your heart.

"Read me your stories with pictures and rhymes.
Read me your poems of woodlands of sweet thyme.
Play rosy-red tunes with the joy of today,
For you are forever in my heart."

Peawee then took out his dock-stem whistle and played the sweet tune again. The twills and rolls of his fingers danced through the notes. Time seemed to stop still: the birds stopped singing, the lonely butterfly closed its wings up, while the insects simply stopped in their tracks. The music eased away in a high note and Peawee put down the whistle.

"My foster mother sang that to me when I went to care for her in the wintertime. It helped me understand her as she drifted in and out of her last dreams. She sang it again as she died in my arms and I seem to have cried ever since. Will the hurting end, Harry?"

Harry thought, what does anyone say to that? It was his senses that brought Harry his wisdom and he needed them now more than ever! Peawee had brought back a part of his foster mother's memory in her song. Her soul had sung to him and he was not alone.

Harry broke the silence. "Lavender blue, Peawee. Please pick me a flower bud of lavender, just the one."

Peawee didn't question Harry's request and quickly flittered over to the lavender beds. He picked out one solitary flower head, almost the same size as his own, and returned to the scarecrow with his load. He climbed up and sat silently on Harry's shoulder, near to the scarecrow's calm face. A breeze rustled through his straw curls, but it was the lavender that came to life.

"Crush the lavender flower in your hands, Peawee, and rub them hard together."

Peawee continued to do as he was told. "Now open your hands wide and let the evening breeze dance across the tiny bud." Harry watched as Peawee silently did so.

"Take a long, deep breath of its fragrance, then another and another." He paused. "Now put the flower to your face and drink of its nature. Try to empty your thoughts and it will help to relax and calm your mind, a simple start to a healing process that will last a lifetime. Whether it be Mother Nature or your own mother, the loss is irreplaceable."

Peawee could only sigh, but he had drunk of the

lavender's goodness. He relaxed and tucked his knees under his chin with his cupped hands placed close to his face. He tipped back his head of hair and inhaled again; still deeper he drew in his breath, filling his tiny lungs and then slowly, ever so slowly, exhaling the spent air across his open lips in a loooong… drawn-out… low… pheeoooooooooow.

Peawee began to understand that his journey would be very hard and lonely at times, and now he needed his friends, the ones who surrounded him with love and told him he would survive it. The lavender was working as he began to take control of his thoughts, but it was impossible to take that step closer and tell Harry the real reason for his deep chagrin. It was too terrible to mention. It made the hurt even more unbearable, but how could he burden someone he loved with that kind of knowledge? It was a knowledge he felt deep down to his very toes. Why was it that he was so often as happy as the daisies in the lawns, but doomed just like their pretty heads are when each week the mechanical mower comes to cut them off in their openness? It leaves the lawn bare and plain, with no flower heads to make daisy chains. Couldn't they simply leave the lawn for a few weeks?

This is how he felt and yet he was trying to be positive, to care for those who needed him. He loved helping them with anything, just like the tales of Harry Also of this wonderful garden and the landscape beyond. Harry's outlook is not like the gardener's as he is pulled in two directions: he must do his job as a scarecrow, but he is also the true storyteller. He wants to express what his characters are thinking, not only what they say. Peawee loved this about Harry, but what would he make of his own darkest story? The story he had been burdened with since a very young Wuidwisp, that was the centre of his dilemma. He turned to Harry.

"I saw a White Hart early this morning, on a knoll. The stag stood proud with the sun streaming through the branches, of the Scots pine, onto his skin. He is young with small antlers and rare to behold. His muscles were tense as his hind quarters pulsated, ready to spring swiftly away at any sign of danger. His hide was pure white, but the sunrise tinged the edges with a clear pink haze. This paled him, but not insignificantly, for he was still dominant standing there. He was a masterpiece. I wanted to reach out and touch his softness. A moment later he was gone, a shadow of the forest, and I was unsure of what I had witnessed. Was he real or in my head? I still don't know."

Harry was glad for this distraction of the sighting. "The white deer is a mystical creature and very rare, but I have heard the gene is in this district," he said. "From time to time a white deer is born and so to actually see a young stag like this is a wonder. Did he speak to you? It is said if the White Hart speaks to you then his countenance will follow you and ease your path."

"It looked deeply at me as if his eyes burned into my soul. But I wasn't afraid, Harry."

"But did he speak to you?" urged the scarecrow.

Peawee's head still rested on his knees and he seemed to be clutching his legs tighter. It took a while, but eventually out of the hush came the words. He was shaking as he said: "The White Hart spoke, he really spoke to me, Harry. 'Come out of your darkness and let your light shine.' That is all he said to me, but my darkness is so deep, Harry, I fear it is bottomless. At times I am at the bottom of a deep well where the sides are so sleek I cannot climb up, even for a true Wuidwisp, and there is no way up into the daylight." It was too much for Peawee and in an instant he had melted away into the darkening day before Harry could press him on the subject.

Peawee was gone again to Handbag Wood, to the shelter of the giant horse-chestnut tree growing amongst the ruins of the ancient traveller's camp, his haven from the outside world. Many years ago the travellers used Handbag Wood as a summer home while working locally on the large estates, mending dry-stane dykes, digging ditches, coppice clearing and such woodland crafts that are all too vanished these days.

Handbag Wood, an unusual name for a small patch of deciduous forest.

Now there is a funny tale, thought Harry, as he recalled many a time he had told this one to the fairy folk in the garden. An elderly gentleman came one day to sit here with Mrs D and recall his childhood on the road as a Scottish Traveller. He was well into his nineties. She asked him if he knew how the wood had got its name, because no-one in the district had the answer. A piece of history, thought lost, had come back to the garden to be remembered.

It was almost at the end of an era up in the woods, the old man said, when these travellers had been replaced by plastic goods, machinery and new methods of working, and so the wood no longer held the romance of these hardy folk and their families, coming each summer to liven up the district and work on the estates. On one of their last summers the air was tinged with sadness, for only a few of the families came to stay in the woods, the woods with no name. He told of one old couple named Joe and Elsie who had spent many happy years staying in the wood. They mended and sewed anything people wanted, patching old coats, replacing worn-out pockets in trousers, mending leather bags as well as shoes. Their pitch had been up near the high road out of the woods, so they didn't have far to walk into town, being elderly now. They had no children of their own, but they always bought sweets for the kids. Elsie was fondly remembered for her engaging, voluptuous smile with no teeth.

Neither of the old couple would have hurt a fly and the wood was a sadder place without them. Some folk have this effect on a place.

A few years after the woodland was abandoned by the travellers, a few families returned for one last summer, just for the hell of it! The trees had grown thick with rhododendrons, making passage almost impossible. However, they did find their old pitch and cleared it for their campfire and canvas tents. Jolly times were had once more but tinged with sadness. The beer flowed freely, the men puffed away on their rolled tobacco and Elsie smoked her pipe while she told stories from the past. Joe had long since died. There had always been dancing and music, but this summer there was only a lone guitar, with ballads of loves lost or a simple waltz.

On their last day, as they packed up to move on, the children went off for one last rummage. They came across Joe's old pitch, where all that remained was a tiny corrugated-iron shed, still standing. It was difficult to get through the dense undergrowth which obliterated the pitch, but eventually they were up beside the tired metal structure. When they tried to open the rickety door they found it jammed by something heavy lying behind it. They put all their weights together and pushed hard at the door.

Eventually the door started to move. They stopped. There was a musty smell coming from inside the shed.

"What happens if it's the body of old Joe?" said one of the kids nervously.

"Ah, don't be silly! It would be mingin' more than this, pal," said the eldest boy. "Come on, let's find oot." They were tough boys and girls; they could cope with anything behind that door! They gave one last almighty heave and the door gave way, and out came a cascade of old handbags.

The old visitor remembered how his young sister had shrilled with delight at the sight of one murky red handbag. She grabbed it for herself and tucked it under her big jumper before someone else could nab it. Later, he recalled how she was to clean it up until it was all shiny new; it even had a pretty brass buckle on the front. Then she wrapped it up and gave it to their mam for Christmas. Their mammy loved it all the more for knowing the hard work her daughter had obviously put into cleaning it up and keeping it a secret.

Naturally the story of the musty handbags rotting away in the woods generated much interest, especially the part where the kids had thought the smell was old Joe himself in his hut! When folk used to ask the travellers where they stayed, the kids always said 'up with the handbags', which eventually became Handbag Wood. The locals started to use the name and over many years the reason, like the rotting handbags themselves, was lost in time.

# Chapter Seven

The garden too was now empty; the lights were on in the Pink House for teatime. Like the growing season here, everything seemed to have such a short time to express itself before it faded like the day. The apple briar's delicate scent of crushed apples would only last a short while on a new morning's breath. A heavy dew was best on the flowers, for this would accentuate the sweet essence of their nectar – then gone, a mystery in a short moment. You have to be quick to capture it. Harry could only hope there would be a breeze to carry this delicacy to him, so he could bathe in it.

Hold on! The garden wasn't empty! The little girl was at the gate, with Teddy under her arm and a rag doll in her hand. She managed to open the gate and with a hop and a skip was at the cherry wood bench. She climbed up and placed teddy and the rag doll beside her. Looking up, she spoke.

"Hallo, Harry Also."

Harry stared blankly to the field beyond.

"I know you can hear me, Harry, because I saw your eyebrows move up and down."

Harry thought he had remained perfectly still and neither eyebrow had moved; he was sure of that. He was the master of statues.

The little girl turned to her toys and gave them a voice. Rags looked at Teddy and spoke first, with a high-pitched squeak.

"Do teddies have eyebrows?" she asked.

Teddy replied in a deep growl of a voice. "No, teddies don't have eyebrows."

There was a pause for thought while they looked at each other, then Teddy added: "Mummies, boys and Dada have eyebrows." Another pause. "But tractors don't have eyebrows."

"Oh!" was all Rags could say to that.

Harry's straw gave a rustle all over; he was chuckling to himself. Little children don't stay still for very long, and sure enough, this little girl was off, gone as soon as her mother called her. As she went off down the path she picked out three weeds from the gravel. It was a habit learnt early; every visitor will pay this toll to the garden and so the path remains clear of weeds. Sorted!

Button-box returned to roost; he looked tired. "It has been a long day Harry," he said. "The fairies and Wuidwisps of Handbag Wood are to organise a gathering, to welcome Peawee back after his long absence. They thought it best to wait a week or so until he is comfortable with the idea of this thanksgiving, when he feels more inclined. It is a glorious time of the year for a celebration of life. All the colours in the trees will be perfect and the water fairies will decorate the grottos. Peawee can only feel the love."

"I worry for him, Button-box – he is soaked in it all."

"Soaked in what, Harry?" asked the crow.

"He is drenched in his grief and I fear the sadness will win. Maybe, just maybe, the fairies can help their friend with their special magic."

It started to rain, pit-a-pat drops on the gravel, faster and faster they fell until the soil changed colours and clenched the moisture within. The plants could drink deeply this night and Jake would be happy he needn't water them tomorrow. The grottos would run freely as the cataracts would not be dry.

Tomorrow was not far away, as the longest day had passed by a couple of weeks back. Harry always looked forward to another day in the vegetable garden, but there wasn't much time to rest his thoughts. This time of year Jake would be able to fill the baskets with plenty of soft fruit and goodies for the Pink House as well as giving surplus to neighbours, friends and visitors.

Harry could hear the long, melodious notes of Peawee's whistle carried from the treetops. He had found his way to deal with the moment and make music, sometimes jolly jigs and reels, but at other times slow ballads from the shores of time. Harry must discipline himself now or he won't have the energy for the next day's happenings. He was listening to silence, a sense of absolute for the scarecrow, now he could ease from one day into the next. He would put his mind to Peawee tomorrow, but now he must rest.

That was quick! An odd sensation, this waiting for the moment of waking up. It was a misty morning, now the rain had stopped, and the air's droplets were distorting the birdsong that came with dawn. Robins and song thrush started the chorus, chaffinches, sparrows, blue tits, blackbirds and, oh yes, there he goes!

"*Cock-a-doodle-dooooo!*" bellowed the rooster.

Harry was just wondering who would visit his patch on this new day when he heard a car start up, doors bang shut and a roar of the engine, as the car sped up the drive. All a bit early, thought Harry, as he could barely make out real shapes yet. The lights had come on in the Pink House, the rooster crowed again and Button-box flew off in a huff at this disturbance. Not long afterwards Mrs D came out to feed the hens, which was unusual, as it was Dolly's job to tend to the hens and collect the eggs each morning.

Mrs D made her way through the garden. "Good morning, Harry, dear," she greeted warmly. "It will be a wonderful day today!" She walked on by with a big smile, only stopping to pick and munch on some of the delicious alpine strawberries. She scrunched up her eyes with the sweetness. "Yum, a summer breakfast feast."

Harry noticed that Mrs D had forgotten the egg basket in her haste. However, she still went inside the large henhouse just outside the garden, where all the hens appeared through the poop hole, followed by the large white rooster. They were soon scratching and scraping around in the undergrowth of the orchard. A few moments later Mrs D was back at Harry's side, but this time there was something different about her. She still had the same boots on, two of them, and a floppy rain hat. What had he missed? She was wearing her large jumper. Oh, that's it! She had pulled up the front hem of the jumper and doubled it over to make an impromptu basket into which she had placed all the eggs, at least two dozen eggs, now bulging out all around her waist. It was just like the frog laying her eggs in a huge puddle, one wet spring here in the field – Harry could see the frog surrounded by all her spawn just like this image of Mrs D surrounded by the hens' eggs. What a clever way to carry something so precious, when you forgot the basket!

Harry then began to think of all the other birds'

eggs; there couldn't be many left in the nests this time of year. Some nests would already have been abandoned by now. Harry's favourite was the ambitious construction project of the long-tailed tit. It is oval-shaped, pieced together with lichen, moss and cobwebs, and lined with at least a thousand tiny feathers. It must be quite a squeeze in there to raise three or four youngsters! He knew the chicks had all flown the nest, because only the other evening the parents were singing in the colourful cherry tree at the edge of the orchard. They sat side by side on a branch as if waiting for something and then, one by one, the young appeared beside the adult birds until a family of four rested in the tree. But the parents continued to call on and on, and they kept calling, until a third but much smaller young tit emerged from the hedgerow, and the family was complete. Five long-tailed tits all in a row on the branch, and this summer even the smallest had survived.

Some latecomers would still have their brood in the nest like the cuckoo, who randomly lays her single egg in a borrowed nest, hoping the owner will raise the young cuckoo as her own. Then there is the spotted flycatcher who, here at the Pink House, has found the best site of all. She was still sitting and feeding her young because this very small species is a late arrival and starts laying after most migrating birds have begun. This spotted flycatcher had found the perfect spot: the nest was built inside a sculpture! It was a jagged metal sculpture of a tram that 'grows' out of the lawn, no bigger than a shoe box. It tops the tramlines that appear out of the grass as two long, curvaceous lines bending up into the sky. The tram car is open and breezy but warm and dry, where the flycatcher makes her small nest almost entirely of moss and feathers.

A man called George Wyllie made the tram. He installed the tramlines under the turf for many yards to make it stable but wobbly at the same time, to give it movement when touched. But this year no-one was to wibble-wobble the tram as the tiny, well-camouflaged bird hunkered down motionless, unblinking and diligent. Do not disturb this perfect spot! The children had been lectured on not touching it and to keep off the lawn, which seemed to upset one small boy. He kept looking at the grass and then at his feet.

Eventually he plucked up the courage to ask, "But how do we play on the swings if we can't walk on the grass?"

Evidently the lecture had been a little *too* harsh! It was explained properly, so they could at least get to the swings and sandpit.

The owls had definitely fledged, because a squirrel had moved into the hole in the huge beech tree. It cleared out all the old nest and pellets of poo and then made an entirely new base inside. All around the bottom of the tree were bones, old manky feathers and pellets of fur, tiny bones and hair from the little animals the parent owls had fed to their chicks over the summer. The woodland walk always looked fresh after a rain shower and the foxgloves make a tall, colourful display at the very edge. Bumblebees cram themselves into the very heart of each last flower fighting their way into the bell-shaped bloom at the top of the stems, some of which were even the height of Harry.

Tall and proud they stand.

Bumblebees, thought Harry, but where were the butterflies? The herbaceous border and wildflower meadow is in colour now with hoverflies, wasps and bees, but only a few butterflies. They were missing this year, a total lack of these most delicate breaths of perfection, tiny creatures of delight bobbing in the motionless breeze, to tumble amongst the borders. The woodland moths had fared better as Harry had seen his favourite ones, the garden-tiger moth and elephant-hawk moth – both of these are brightly coloured and large members of these whispers of the night. Harry wanted to see the red admirals, the painted lady and the imposing eyes on the peacocks' wings, which stared harder into the light then even his own.

"Oh, where are the butterflies!" cried Harry.

"They will come, Harry, but the hard rains of the last summer leached the goodness out of that season. There were bad flying days, no nectar and life was hard. There are always bad things that get in the way of the good." It was Peawee. In his wisdom he had returned to his friend's side; his dark days were not Harry's fault. "Don't worry, Harry, the orchard fairies will do their magic and nurture as many caterpillars and butterflies as they can. The meadow flowers have had many eggs on the foliage, and some of the nettles are crammed full of caterpillars already. Be patient." Peawee popped down and looked hard into Harry's eyes. "Some would say a scarecrow has a vacant expression," he teased.

"Oh, do they!" retorted Harry. "Well, *not* this one! Nothing will take this smile from my face! It can rain *all* day, sleet, hail or even snow, but I am here whatever the weather while you are tucked up in your feather nest, all nice and cosy."

"Sorry, Harry, I didn't mean to hurt your feelings, it is just that there is something in the air today, something good."

"That's fine, Peawee, I am just glad to see you in such good spirits!" But before Harry could ask the Wuidwisp why his mood had lightened up, Peawee jumped up.

"Well, today will be a wonderful day," he announced. "There is a special happening coming to the garden, just you wait and see, my scarecrow friend." Peawee really was in a good mood.

"Let me guess," said the little furry creature from the land below ground.

"Hallo, Moleskin!" welcomed Harry. "You are up bright and early!"

"Well, with that roaring car this morning I couldn't sleep anymore, so I came up to see what the fuss was. I guess everyone has gone on holiday and left us in peace," said the mole in hope more than anything, as moles like peace and quiet.

"Nope," said Peawee. "Sorry to disappoint you,

Moleskin, but that is the wrong answer. Come on, Harry, you have a guess."

Harry looked around. It must be something very special to bring Peawee out of his glum hole into this better mood. He knew his friend was very good at pretending to be in a better mood than he really was, but this time seemed different, more genuine.

He decided to play along with this game. "Something to do with the fairies in the wood, but I can't think what," he said. "Are they bringing something to the garden?"

Peawee was being mischievous as he danced around the trees. "Nope again, but here comes Jake. He will give you a big clue!" And off the Wuidwisp went, to the top of one of the large cypress trees, while the mole scampered in retreat to his meadow tunnels.

Jake walked through the vegetable garden and spent an hour or so watering the greenhouses, weeding here and there, his usual routine. Everything seemed normal to Harry, but Jake did have a big smile on his face, more so than usual. Harry still had no idea what was going on or what Peawee could possibly be up to. Then Jake did something unusual: he fetched a small bright red bucket and his trusted secateurs and went over to the sweet pea bed, where a long row of sweet peas rambled their way amongst the twigs and netting. Jake started to pick just one colour of sweet pea, quite beautifully ready blooms, while leaving all the other on the plants, and after a few minutes had completely filled the little red bucket with pink and only pink flowers. The scent was overpowering Harry, but he was refreshed by it – you can't beat these lovely new flowers this time of year, he thought. Jake left the garden and whistled all the way back to the Pink House.

Harry could only marvel at the flowers at this time of year, the dazzling midnight blue of the ceanothus as the perfect backing on the brick wall for the tall, silver leaves of the stachys. They're known as lambs' ears because of their shape and soft downy coating, their spikes of small, almost fluorescent red flowers soon fill with bumblebees and the whole plant hums.

Of course, here in the vegetable garden the harvests were well on their way, with a mass of broad beans to pick. Jake would harvest them into the wheelbarrow and deliver them to the Pink House, to be podded from their downy soft pods and frozen for the wintertime. However, some of the extra-special little ones were always eaten cooked fresh, with a little butter on the top. Harry delighted in all the vegetables, salad crops of all shapes and colours, herbs to add to the spread, new potatoes thick with mint flakes on top as the butter melted down their little spheres. There were carrots, cucumbers, beetroot, but the sweetcorn would be in the ground just a little longer. It was one of the 'disasters' last year as the cold rain was relentless and the corn failed. Harry would marvel at some of the strange names to vegetables like aubergine, growing in the greenhouse, parsnip, cauliflower, kohlrabi, asparagus and pumpkin – not only did this sound amazing, but what a huge masterpiece of orange magic!

Harry was just looking at the bed of artichokes with their flower stems almost up to his chin and soon to be picked, when Peawee emerged from his hiding place.

"Now do you see, Harry?" he called. "Look, pink sweet peas, and over there Mrs D is blowing up pink balloons and tying them to the railings of the fence line, all the way up the avenue."

Harry couldn't concentrate. The garden had taken over his mind in raptures of sorrow and then delight, senses unspoken of. Maybe the fairies had spread a magic dusting to confuse his thoughts – at times the only thing he grew in this garden was tired!

"Oh, Harry!" Peawee was becoming exasperated with his friend. He hung down off Harry's bonnet onto his nose and sat there. He gave a big sigh.

Oh, dear, that was a bad idea; Peawee had tickled Harry's nose and he… was… going… to… *aaaaaaah-tichoo!* The sneeze seemed to have dislodged some dust from Harry's thinking.

"It's a girl!" he cried. "Way-hey! It's another girl, born to Dolly and farmer William!"

If it had been windy enough Harry would have tried to spin on his pole with joy. Have you ever seen a scarecrow spinning round?

"That's marvellous, Peawee. Now that *is* a special happening, and the balloons make a wonderful homecoming. I can't wait to see the little baby in her pram here in the garden. Oh, I could hug a tree!"

# Chapter Eight

A tenacious young orchard fairy whistled down to the friends; he was hiding in the ivy growing up the wall. Peawee looked about them and whistled back a sign that all was safe to come down to them. The fairy floated down and settled on Harry's shoulder.

He was dressed all in dazzling white, with a tough little white hat on his head.

"Hallo, Peardrop," said Harry, "it is lovely to see you here in the garden."

"Hallo, Harry. Thank you, it is lovely to be here in this amazing vegetable patch. What a fantastic summer we are having and such wonderful news about the baby girl born today." The fairy got up and gave a little twirl of delight on one tiptoe.

"I must agree," said Peawee.

"All of the woodland folk are in a frenzy – there is quite a buzz up in Handbag Wood," continued Peardrop. "I have been given the task by Oobit, our tree-fairy elder, to come and invite Peawee to Handbag Wood for a thanksgiving in memory of his foster mother. We could also celebrate the new girl child. One life ends as another life begins, just like the seasons. Do you like the idea?"

Peawee seemed agitated. "But what of Harry? He could never get to Handbag Wood and I must have my best friend with me, otherwise what is the point." Peawee was suddenly pulled down into a dark place with all his thoughts of death. He didn't know why it could happen so quickly on such a lovely day as this one. A horrible silence with a hollow emptiness in the pit of his stomach was all he felt. He didn't know what to do.

"I don't mean to be ungrateful, Peardrop," he blurted out, "but I don't think it is a good idea just now, maybe another time." Before anyone had time to persuade him otherwise, Peawee was gone.

"Oh, dear, what have I said?" Peardrop was genuinely upset. He hadn't meant to hurt Peawee's feelings; he had meant to cheer him up. Everyone had noticed how sad he was feeling.

Harry tried to comfort the orchard fairy. "It will be alright – he sometimes just goes away like that, don't worry. Give him time and then I am sure he will join you all for the celebration."

"There is only one thing to do, then," said Peardrop.

"What can that be?" asked Harry.

"I will tell the elders that the celebration must come to you, Harry, to this garden, so Peawee's bestest friend can be with him. You tell him from me, Harry, as soon as you can. Try to convince him it will all be OK with his friends and we won't make a fuss. We can just have a small gathering."

With that statement Peardrop was gone. As quickly as his wings beat he danced off into the orchard, past the fruit trees and up to Handbag Wood. He was now on a mission.

Harry had no idea when Peawee would return. He couldn't understand what was in Peawee's mind; something was most definitely stopping the Wuidwisp from expressing himself. It had all started out so well this new day, but as events happen, the day can quickly change. Life is no different to gardening, Harry thought, it can be a delight or a scourge with idyllic blue skies and a gentle breeze, but then it can suddenly change to tempestuous weather. Crops can be shredded in one cruel downpour of hail or flattened by heavy rain.

Harry was glad to hear the clinch of the gate once

more and Jake's return; it meant that a sense of normality and discipline could prevail and calm his shaken soul. A few seconds later two of the children appeared, but they had forgotten something.

"Shut that gate, please!" shouted Jake. "And don't forget your three weeds!" he added, with a chuckle.

Jake loved the children coming to the vegetable garden; he believed in the next generation understanding what people did here. You can buy flowers and fresh vegetables and pretend, but there is nothing like working the soil. So, get out there into the garden, however large or small, be it your own or someone else's, an allotment or a window box, a balcony or a patio – just do it! He always wanted to make the children feel involved and gave them tasks with a small reward afterwards, say strawberries, a crisp bean to snap and eat, or Mrs D would produce her special scones with homemade jam for tea. There was even a small area of cut grass next to the brick wall where they could spread a large blanket and have a picnic. He wanted them to realise early on in life that the gardener's finesse was a closeness to the soil that equalled an intensity and could very quickly become an obsession. The balance came with experience and the joy with success.

For now Jake had work to do and little hands to keep busy. He set Hamish, the eldest boy, to cleaning up Harry. He gave him a small sponge and the red bucket full of warm water. "Just wash away the dust and smarten up Harry Also, in celebration of the new baby's coming home," said Jake, and then he sat the other very young girl down on the tiny wicker chair just inside the greenhouse. She sat very still and watched as Jake meticulously watered the tomatoes and aubergines, for the second time in the day, as it had been so hot.

"Now for the smelly water!" he exclaimed.

"Oh no!" said the children, giggling with fun.

Oh no! thought Harry.

"That is the worst job *in the world*. Can we go now?" said the boy.

"No, no, come on. It isn't that bad!" said Jake, and fetched the watering cans.

They walked up to a large, green water butt. "Better you pinch your noses, kids!" He took the lid off the butt and the children all stood in a line, holding their noses. Slowly Jake lifted the lid, releasing the most revolting, rotting smell *ever* from the water. "Yuck yucketty yuck," the little girl said, when she wasn't quite quick enough to cover her nose. She stepped back away from the water butt. "Why is it *so* smelly, Jake, and what is it for?"

"It is called comfrey water. We cut lots of comfrey leaves in the late spring, put them in a string bag with a heavy stone and then into this butt of water to rot down. During the summer we dilute this smelly liquid with water and have an organic feed for the runner beans, sweetcorn or even the flowerbeds. There is one very important thing to remember, though."

"What is that, Jake?" asked the girl.

"Remember to wear gloves or your hands will smell

of it for days!" They all laughed, happy in their work.

Harry was safe; they had gone down the garden to the bean trench and taken the smelly water with them. He was looking very smart after his wash and brush-up. The boy had done a great job and even managed to top Harry's hat with an ox-eyed daisy.

Hamish joined Jake and the girl while they gathered some vegetables, happy that he didn't need to wear gloves now. Jake believed in feeling the soil between your fingers and not covering up that most precious of senses, feeling the 'snap' of the pea pods, the delicate softness of the strawberry and the jaggedness of the gooseberry, all part of the fun. He had even learnt how to pick the early leaves of the nettle plants, to make tea or soup – no gloves, as long as you're careful. All skills to be learnt here in the garden. With the baskets full, the trio went back to the Pink House, refreshed and laden with goodies.

Peace returned, as did Button-box.

"Good to see you, Button-box," said Harry.

"*Craw-craw*," replied the curious crow. "Good to see you too, Harry, but I only saw you this morning. What's up?"

"Can you fetch Peawee? Tell him there will be no party without me, so he can relax."

"A party! What, where, when?" demanded the crow.

Harry told Button-box the whole story and the crow seemed a little peeved with Peawee's antics. A party would be fun.

"I will find him and give him a gruff. The fairies

are trying to cheer him up and he is being ungrateful. I think he is being rude." Button-box was being very firm, but Harry calmed him down and told him to be gentle towards the Wuidwisp, or they may lose him forever. At that the bird flew away, consoled and in better spirits, to find their friend.

It didn't take long before Peawee was back on Harry's shoulder, but he seemed distraught and all mixed up. Harry always knew what to say on these occasions and it felt like a giant hug when he did so.

"Come to the garden, Peawee, and believe in the good in the world, my sweet friend. Sometimes it is all we have." The crow had not joined them and the silence was unbearable, but Harry had the patience for anything.

There was no tune from the stem whistle or song in his heart, but eventually Peawee came close to Harry's ear. He didn't turn his head but leant against his friend's cheek. "It wasn't my foster mother who died, Harry," he whispered. "It was my mother."

An icy shiver went down Harry's back as he felt numbed by this revelation. Had he heard correctly? Was it Peawee's mother who had died? That couldn't be right. He spoke very softly. "That would make you a wood fairy and you are a Wuidwisp. How could you be a fairy, Peawee? You have no wings."

# Part Three

# Autumn

# Chapter Nine

*Stop!* I want to get off! Time and space were spinning, revolving out of control, and there was nothing Harry could do about the chain of events already written down. He could not alter the past. His arms were spread wide open, not to scare things away from the garden but to embrace them. In all reality he couldn't say boo to a goose; he was an illusion.

Stop feeling so sorry for yourself, Harry thought. He was angry with himself at the effect of what Peawee had told him. Now was not the time to get annoyed; he would simply reorder his thoughts, take a deep breath and be there for Peawee. The young Wuidwisp – or should he say fairy? – his best friend, was away up in the tall softness of the wellingtonia's treetop, up in the mists of fortune. Peawee had curled up and slept in Harry's pocket soon after admitting he was in fact a wood fairy. He rose very early the next morning, apologising to Harry and leaving without a reply. It was part of his character and now Harry understood so much more about it. There was a wickedness in there, a very sad tale that Peawee was yet to tell, but he would be back. Harry now knew that Peawee was going to tell him everything.

For now the seasons were racing onwards and the hay was to be cut. William was already out on his old tractor cutting the last field. The other larger field had been cut and baled a week ago but this second one was to be made into hay the old-fashioned way, by hand. There were beautiful grasses here in the field. Some of them had fabulous names like cocksfoot and fescues, timothy and Yorkshire fog. Harry didn't get to see the other shires of the country, but he could now imagine what the fog looked like in Yorkshire!

The only task to be completed with the tractor was to cut the long grass with the old sickle-bar mower. William liked using the vintage tractors and farm equipment; he had grown up using these mechanical wonders. He loved the feel and roundness of them. One tractor was so old it had no cab, a metal 'bucket' seat with holes to let the rainwater through and a large exhaust pipe on top of the engine block. She was a beautiful smooth grey colour and was called Fergy. These masters of the past allowed time to drift, some would say in a stupid way. Why not move forward with the bigger, faster machines? But here at the farm life was to move in a calmer way, and that was why William and Dolly had come to the farm in the first place. They were here to work the land in an organic, mixed-farming environment, caring for the land and all within it. Animals as well as vegetables were all raised to feed the community. William's father had been a ploughman before him, but he had used the large Clydesdale horses to pull the plough in his day. He still trained new stock for agricultural shows and ploughing matches and hours were spent just braiding their tails and manes with colourful ribbons, with shiny brass plates on their tack.

The next morning, after the cut hay had wilted and the ground had dried out a little, the gang would appear. Everyone who wanted to join in was encouraged to take up a wooden hay rake or pitchfork and help. The first couple of days the hay was turned over and spread out by these hearty followers of a bygone era. It was the rhythm that captivated Harry: swish to the left, swish to the right – whoosh! up into the air. In the evening it was all bunched up into long rows, as the hay was kept drier this way during the night and early dew of dawn. With a large wooden rake in their hands the folk would almost make a dance of it as they swayed back and forth, grabbing and piling the hay up in front of them, all moving along the row at the same pace and rhythm with small sideways steps. Next morning the sun would dry the earth between the rows and later they spread it out once more in the same rhythm, the same dance. People wanted this experience, this fellowship. They also liked the idea of helping so many insects, the small mammals, and the frogs and toads hiding in the meadow. Even the sticky slugs were safe there – the hay was not cut low, which helped!

Harry knew that hay time was difficult for the bugs that lived in the fields, but the hay had to be made. He had two favourite insects: the wasp beetle because the pattern on its back was black and white to make the birds think he was a wasp, and the other was the florescent-green golden weevil. Oh, and don't forget the ladybirds, those little green tortoise beetles who lived on the white dead nettle, and so many more! He really couldn't choose now.

It was the perfect summer for it. The sun was hot and healing this year and soon the hay was gathered in. It had to be very dry before it was tossed onto the trailer and stacked loosely in the old barn. There were many sounds of laughter that day as the folk played amongst the hay – don't fall off the top! It could be dusty too, so the ladies wore scarves around their heads, and from a distance they looked like a mass of brightly coloured flower heads in the field. On these sunny days the strawberry cream teas were a way of saying thanks to everyone who turned up to help. Mrs D baked the best scones ever and homemade jam topped the bill. The hay smelled so sweet, Harry wished he could eat it like the sheep did – his straw never smelt like that, even when he was re-stuffed with new straw.

Around the edges of the barley and hay fields was an area always left for the wildflowers to grow, and for creatures living on the edge. It was an environment lost on many larger farms these days, filled with poppies, ox-eye daisies, cornflowers, wild gladioli, campion and so many other delicate wildflowers; they made Harry's head spin in delight. He could see beyond the garden next to the orchard, to this variable rainbow of swaying, tiny dots of colour. At the bottom of the field in the shade of some trees was a damp area for the orchids, trumpets of purple and green, and a haven for the orchid fairy. The children of the Pink House had even built a fairy playground for them, a small log cabin, platforms of twigs and moss, and even a flying fox set up between two small trees! The fairies loved it.

Best of all were the butterflies. They had arrived and were everywhere now, a veritable revolution in the garden. They were hungry for life, such a short time to be, and desperate for the nectar of every single plant they visited. He couldn't believe the variety in these graceful creatures, the dusty brown fritillaries, the common blues and his favourite larger peacocks and admirals. Jake now spent most mornings amongst the brassicas collecting the caterpillars of the cabbage whites – if he didn't do this they would simply munch their way through all the cabbages, cauliflowers and broccoli plants in his garden and quickly reduce them to a sorry sight. He would squish the yellow eggs hiding on the underside of the leaves, better than using nasty chemicals, and he would take any caterpillars he found to the huge compost area where he would lay down some cabbage leaves for them. The children would also put some in a large open jar with cabbage leaves and watch the caterpillars grow, then harden to a chrysalis and a few weeks later, if they were lucky, watch the new butterfly emerge from the shell. This was a magical moment easily missed, but if they were patient they would be rewarded.

Each season brings its own pressures and Harry's only outlet was to feel his body drift away out of control. He did this at any time of the day or night and he was doing it now. One moment he was up with the stars, but that was too arid. Then he'd be in a river, his body poised against water, struggling with the current. The very act was giving meaning to 'walking through water', something he had never done but somehow he knew what it felt like. He was sure he had been there catching a moment's glance of the lead-glazed blues of the kingfisher, flying relentlessly up along the riverbank. A dash... a flash... gone.

He could sense the people from the past who had lived here or just passed by.

He came to know this garden and land about him closely, and it intensified his views. Gardening is true to life; it is not about growing the biggest, heaviest vegetables because invariably the smaller fruit are the sweetest. All about him were the swivelling, darting swallows and martins. From high in the sky they would dive down, as if in a game, totally lost in their fun. It seemed an exaggeration, an unnecessary burst of energy, just to swim magically in the air above the barley heads now golden and top-heavy. But these tiny birds, with gaping mouths, were taking their fill of the small flies hovering in the humid air just centimetres above the corn crops. With perfect precision, they became acrobats of the air. Harry felt he could bounce on the barley crop as it spread like an eider-down duvet across the field.

The air was still, incredibly still. Silent. There was never true silence in Harry's world. It was always babbling, alive even when asleep. Late summer nights could seem empty, but they still contained light. Suddenly he was startled by the sound of a gurgling baby as a cherished group entered the garden; the new baby was on her first outing to the vegetable garden with her sister, mummy and dada. The evening sun highlighted the family as they sat on the cherry bench.

"Say hallo to Harry, Dada. He will understand you – he understands everyone."

William gave a huge smile to his daughter but shook his head.

"Please, Dada, or he will be upset."

"O-ay," said William. "He-oo Hawee, how are uoo?"

"He says he is very well," said Rose quite seriously, "and he thanks you for asking." Happy with the outcome, she skipped off to play with her toy tractor in the fine gravel.

Harry loved this family and many a time he told the tale of how they came to be here. Dolly, the mum, had met William while on holiday, when she was an au pair for a banker and his family from London. She had never been to the countryside before and instantly fell in love with it, and more importantly with William. He was the ploughman on the farm and was quiet and introverted, seldom speaking a word. He had the most generous of smiles Dolly had ever seen, his whole face beamed when they met, but she didn't realise at the time that it was for her and only her that he did this.

Dolly would talk away nervously to William and he would nod and smile, or simply nibble on his words.

Nothing about William seemed to bother Dolly and they had a wonderful summer together; it was meant to be. Dolly seemed to understand him, which confused the ploughman as he had been born with a cleft palate – his tongue could not form sounds that needed the roof of the mouth. Although he had an operation to restore the gap in the roof of his mouth he still could not articulate his words properly and most people found it hard to understand him, but he made the best of it and used sign language when he needed to. They were married the next summer and now, here they were, with their small family living a life they believed in, with people who believed in them. It was hard work but worth every moment, even in the pouring rain!

William unwrapped a toffee and popped it into the little girl's mouth, then did the same for Dolly and himself. He took his family back down the path, through the iron gate and home to their cottage. A ripple of contentment whistled across Harry's face.

A large, bedraggled black feather zigzagged past Harry's nose. He didn't sneeze, but it did alert him to the arrival of Button-box.

"Hallo, old scarecrow," teased Button-box.

"Less of the 'old', thank you very much. You are not looking so good yourself, old crow, a few bits missing, I see," replied Harry.

"I hate moulting time and this year, for some reason, I am late." Button-box had literally collapsed onto Harry's shoulder, his approach to landing somewhat askew. He was just a little peeved and busied himself preening the feathers on the pinions of his wings. He had to be patient now, as the new feathers grew in. At least they didn't all fall out at once like some of the hens' feathers did until they were almost bald, but of course they couldn't fly anyway. He would soon be back to his shiny self. "Now what did I come to tell you? Oh, yes! Peardrop has organised with the elders of Handbag Wood that they will bring the party here to the vegetable garden. They were sure Peawee would now come. Have you seen him lately?"

"He is about – he will talk when he is ready." Harry tolerated the crow's incessant nibbling at his feathers; after all, it must be very itchy when the new feathers come through.

The scarecrow and his companion now relished the end of the day, happy in each other's company of the twilight. In the evening air someone was playing the piano up at the Pink House. The melody drifted towards them, laden with pearls of sweetness, a slow rhythm of tiny notes to fill the air. A slow ascent in the melody raised it, then down again, growing softer and softer. Up it went again on a twill in the song so sweet, it almost made Harry cry – was it a waltz? At the very end it seemed to say goodbye all by itself, from one distinct high note to then fall away up and down to a silent close. Harry knew it was a piece by the composer Chopin and was called Nocturne No 2, because it was Mrs D's favourite piece that she played, and many a time she would whistle it in the garden and then comment on how calm it made her feel. Her mother had used to play it to her when she was a little girl.

There was something, maybe a spiritual antidote, about piano music played near an open window. It seemed to travel forever on a healing path. Just as the piece finished another soft, even softer sound filtered down. It was the same melody only played on a different instrument, the doleful sound of Peawee's whistle.

# Chapter Ten

Harry could see farther than any human being; he had a contract with the horizon. His hearing was no different. He was never confused by the direction the sounds were coming from and the amount of information they held. All his energies were focused on the senses of sight and sound. Still the music hit him like a feather brushing against skin on a breathless day. Over and over again the melody of Chopin dissected his thoughts. Take your time, Peawee, he thought, I will be here when you need me. It was now he needed him. Peawee came from the song to be at Harry side.

"*Craw-craw, craw-craw*. What's up with the Wuidwisp then, or are you not talking to us? Maybe I should go? I can tell I am not wanted!"

"No, Button-box, I need to tell you both my tale," said Peawee, as he stared straight ahead of him for fear of not speaking the truth. "I need to tell you how I lost my wings and survived. To this day no-one, but no-one, knows."

"Lost your wings!" exclaimed Button-box. "But—"

"Shut up, crow," interrupted Harry. "Just sit there and shut up. Let Peawee say his piece in peace and then we may actually understand something."

The crow ruffled his shabby feathers and hunched his shoulders in submission.

He just knew not to say another word.

Peawee fidgeted nervously. This was going to be hard, very hard, and the jovial crow didn't make life any easier. Should he go on? Would they understand? Or would they simply laugh and judge him harshly, or even, worst of all, not believe him? He couldn't bear that. He got up as if to leave.

"Peawee!" pleaded Harry. There was nothing but ashen emptiness. "Please stay, take your time. These things need to be said."

Peawee had grown thin and his facial features ran dry like the riverbed in a hot summer. His cheeks, normally chubby, were now gaunt. He had not been eating. The only reality important to Peawee right now was the reality in his mind. He didn't want to be an onlooker anymore; he had to enter the stage and tell all. It had to start now.

"We will still be here," continued Harry. "Take that step. We have all night and we have all the stars to guide us to the moon and back. Image you are weightless but travelling at thousands of feet a second. You disappear around the other side of the moon and come back a couple of minutes later, darkness… then light… and we are still here. If there is something in your way, Peawee, go through it or round it, but do it."

"I just want you guys to understand why I am 'me'."

"We are listening," said Harry.

"Yes, we are, me too, I mean, I too, or is it… *craw-craw!*"

Harry gave the crow a stern look and then a wink. He knew his feathered friend was trying his best to help Peawee, but now was the time for, 'Stop! Listen… what do you hear?'

Peawee gingerly returned to Harry's shoulder. His throat was dry. Harry rubbed his cheek warmly against Peawee. "Start at the beginning, my friend, and we will be with you until the end."

There was a pause and then Peawee relaxed, unafraid now and at ease. "When I was a very young woodland fairy we lived over near the west coast, in a forest of large horse chestnut trees, elm and a few giant oaks. In early summer the pathways into the wood were covered in wild garlic and lily of the valley. There were ancient stone circles nearby and fields of cattle and sheep. Life was good for us. One day there was a festival with music and dancing for all the woodland fairies and Wuidwisps. Most of the folk were in a clearing having a good time. My parents were dancing, and my mother would look back for me every now and again to give me a big smile. It was winter and I remember playing all by myself by a fountain. It was set back from the clearing in pallid darkness. The water cascaded out into the air and tiny droplets, landing on the stones thereabout, soon turned to icicles, for it was very cold. I was mesmerised by the sounds and my reflection in the ice.

"I loved everything about the forest with all its seasonal changes, but in one ugly moment my life was to be shattered. From out of the backdrop a gruff voice talked smoothly to me. I couldn't see who it was, but I was drawn towards this shape. 'Would you like me to break you off an ice crystal and you can taste it?' said the voice. I still couldn't see who it was but thought him part of the crowd of friends. He seemed kind enough, so I accepted his offer, and he slowly emerged from the night shadows. It was then that I felt a chill within me and I turned to go to my mother. She was there, just over there."

Peawee had stopped. He held out his hand to motion

somewhere out there. He sighed, dropped his hand and continued.

"His eyes were made of clinker and his face like dry onion leaves. I could see the grime in the folds of his skin on his naked torso and slime around his neck. His mouth screwed up as he champed on a roasted pinecone. He then spat out the hard seed pods, and globs of green saliva oozed down his chin. He came right up to me, snapped off a small icicle and held it to my mouth. Brushing it across my lips, he said, 'Now taste it.' I then knew what fear was and I turned to fly away, but he caught me just as I left the ground. He quickly placed one of his huge, bony hands over my mouth and dragged me into the deep overhang of branches in the cold undergrowth."

Peawee was trembling now as the fear of loss overwhelmed him. He bent his head down between his knees and fell silent. A surge of nausea came to his throat. Button-box flew up and back down beside Peawee; he opened his wing and Peawee instinctively moved under it. The healing had to start here.

He continued, "Then the pain, I didn't understand what was happening. I tried to fight back, but he told me not to move or he would hurt my mother too." Tears came and fell down Peawee's face. They were pearls of lament.

"You don't have to—" said Harry.

"Yes! I do!" cried Peawee. "I do… I must… I do have to tell you." He turned his head towards Harry and, placing his chin on his hunched-up knees, he spoke on. "I will never forget the smell of his acrid breath. He was drunk on pied juice and ramshackled smokes. His hands tore at my jacket, vest and then at the heart of my wings. In one swift movement my wings were ripped out of my back and he opened his disgusting mouth and ate them. I couldn't scream; I couldn't even move as the pain descended into my very core. Then, as quickly as he'd come, the ugly brute was gone and I was left on the ice-cold earth. Suddenly my mother appeared and I will never forget her face as a silent scream came from her open mouth. Then the sound came and a rush of wings appeared from everywhere. 'It's the Droigs,' they cried. I didn't know what a Droig was; all I knew was the pain. In my heart I wasn't alive anymore and the world I had known was gone. My life was ebbing further away and I found it hard to breathe. I was dying."

Peawee was clasping his hands so tightly, the knuckles were cold and turning white. He placed them up to his lips as a comfort and to warm them. He didn't think he could continue with this tale and wished he had died out there by the fountain.

Harry felt Peawee withdraw as the crow held him tightly under his wing; he was numbed by the revelation and his vision blurred. In front of him was the garlic and onion beds. The onion tops had been folded over to dry out for storage in neat rows, like rail tracks disappearing into the distance, all fading in the dusk. The dry, wrinkled skin of the onions only made him see the Droig's skin.

Harry had heard of the Droigs once before and never a good thing was said of them. They were from the Fractions, the outer limits of the cities, where the lamplights glowed all night and wastelands never slept, human rubbish stank and low-lives came out to play. They only left their territories for mischief and crime, and their biggest thrill was to eat the wings of very young fairies. He had never met a fairy who had encountered one, so the Droigs had never been part of his thinking, until now. He was desperate to hear more, but could Peawee manage to tell the end of the tale, or would the memories drag him under?

The shaking in Peawee's thin body had stopped. Button-box gave Harry a wizened look as his eyes filled with desperate tears. This must be gruelling for his friend.

"I dreamt I saw you guys standing by my side and whispering my name. I needed to return then and explain, and only then could I live free of this horror." Peawee journeyed deeper into his experience but refused to be hard on himself any longer.

"But how did you heal and not die? How did you become a Wuidwisp?" Curiosity now consumed Harry and he wasn't ashamed of his questioning; after all, this was what Peawee had come to tell them. If it was too hard to go on then it didn't matter, but for now this was his only option.

"When I awoke I was in my mother's arms," said Peawee. "Instinct had overtaken her misery and she took me to the healing witch fairy. The life waters were draining from my tiny body, but she stemmed the flow with a poultice of herbs. Comfrey was then placed on the open wound and packed tightly. A broth of ajuga, sage and rosemary was cooked, but I remember I just couldn't drink the liquid. My mother came to my side and with her deep maternal love she took up the bowl and drew into her mouth some of the warm broth. She then came to my lips and placed her mouth on mine. I tasted the herbs, the seasoning and life-giving broth. Again, as if at her breast, she was feeding me, encouraging me with every sound and motion in her heart. A kiss of life. How could I resist? I had to try if only for her. I remember falling into a deep sleep, unsure if I would return, but knowing if I did I would no longer be that wood fairy playing innocently at the fountain, or up in the trees."

Darkness came early that night in the garden and the three friends slept uneasily.

They were together and yet alone in their thoughts, vulnerable but safe in each other's arms. The crow's down kept Peawee safe and warm, until he too eventually slept. "*Craw-craw*," and the bird was pleased. Tomorrow could come now and they would battle the remainder of the story together in a new light.

Harry was the first to wake, never really sleeping. The glow of the big city beyond the Campsies only highlighted the revulsion he now felt. He had such visions. He tried hard to find ordinary words, or a sentence to say what was on his mind, but to balance these thoughts was impossible. He desperately sought an answer. Why, Peawee, why do Droigs eat fairy wings for fun? Why are families shattered apart? His head was spinning. He shook and got his balance back.

Peawee emerged from under the black wing into the morning. He stretched up and flew into the evergreen, where he sat awhile, before taking his whistle and playing.

This time he offered a tune of whimsical surprise. Harry looked at Button-box and Button-box looked back, just as amazed.

"Are you guys all right?" asked Peawee from the tree.

"What do you mean, 'are we all right'? It is us who should be asking you that question!" replied the crow.

"I have been living with this all my life, but it must have been hard for you to hear the tale. I don't expect anyone to understand and that is ultimately why my mother then did what she did. So I will continue my story, but don't judge her badly, please."

"We would never do that, my friend," replied Harry, settling his straw to listen once more.

Peawee took up his position next to Harry. He had all the time in the world as the Pink House was still in darkness. "I promised my mother I wouldn't tell anyone this sad story until she died. She was to spend the rest of her life waking each day to the vision of the horror. It eased over time, but she always felt a deep sense of guilt for leaving me to play alone on the edge of the forest. My own guilt is deep, rotted with anxiety and self-hatred as I long believed it was all my fault, so I couldn't tell anyone anyway."

"But surely the only one to blame is the Droig," interrupted Harry.

"Yes, but tell a small wood fairy that when he is drowning in pain, mistrust and disbelief."

"I'm sorry, I didn't want to sound flippant."

"No! No, don't you say that, Harry! I know you both must be feeling awful, dislodged and sad. Maybe I should stop altogether."

"Yeah, right, just when you were telling us how you got on with your lives and leave us sitting on the end of our perches!" Trust Button-box to ease the moment, but at least it made them all smile. There was nothing funny about any of this tale, but at least they could relax a little in each other's company.

Peawee continued. "My father and a group of the woodland folk swiftly followed the trail of the Droig. He wasn't hard to track: his smell was everywhere and the slime around his body left a sticky trail. I later learned that they had cornered the Droig, who was contempt in the cruellest manner. He laughed at them and told them I tasted sweet. My father, normally a quiet, gentle elder, flew at him in a rage of despair and they were locked in a mass of flailing arms, wings and grime. Near a waterfall where the winter's cold had descended like a stone, the two thundered at each other until, slipping on the sheet ice at the top, they plunged to the foot of the waterfall. The Droig managed to grab my father's wings and they were pulled from his body, ripped away in a raw act of degenerate finality. At the moment of impact on the ice below a large icicle loosened from a shelf above them and fell, to pierce the top of the skull of the Droig. His body floated away, a heap of screaming wretchedness. My father was dragged from the cold waters and died in his friends' arms. He had been lost by the family he loved and who loved him. My mother and I were now alone."

"How long did it take for your wounds to heal?" asked Harry. "I thought fairies with no wings never survived. And why the Wuidwisp disguise?"

"My first memory was a strange sensation as the life poured back, and I took a gulp of air. My mouth was dry and I could feel my heart beating – no, it was *pounding* in my chest. The visions in my head disturbed any sleeping moment and I was too weak to even crawl. The witch fairy warned my mother that if the Droigs learned that I had lived, they would come back for us and serve their revenge in whichever way they wanted. It would not be pleasant either; they have evil habits and death is never far away. As soon as I was able to be moved my mother bundled me up, strapped me to her side and flew away. She didn't stop until the forest was out of sight. She just had to leave the area, distance herself and me from the hell therein and the return of the Droigs. She didn't tell any of her elders where she was going. It was just her and me. I had no concept of time and distance – they were irrelevant anyways as the past and the future had lost meaning."

Harry stopped his friend from continuing his story.

He saw the colour was draining from his body. "Peawee, you need to rest and forage. Your skin is too pale and you need to feed the fire in your belly to face this new day." Peawee tried to argue, but Harry was bold in his defence. "You may have taken the first step in your recovery, but without energy your body will fade and – more importantly – the mind will become weak with despair. Go now, don't presume you have the strength without the nourishment. We will be here when you return. The Pink House is waking and soon Jake will arrive to care for his garden. Go! Before I get really mad!"

"But, Harry, you never get mad, you leave that to Button-box!" The three friends laughed, a little nervously. Button-box ruffled his body awake and flew up into his day – for once the crow was speechless and needed to clear his head.

Harry's concern was written on his face and he couldn't hide the worry. Peawee noticed and stretched his thin legs. "I'll be fine, Harry. You are right in that I must go and visit my trees to take in their energy and love. I'll hug one for you too. Don't worry, we can spend time together. I must answer your questions as there is no going back. There is no use in pretending my fears are not there, either in my nightmares or in my waking adventures. I must do this for my mother's sake."

"And your own," Harry was quick to add.

Peawee managed a smile before jumping onto Harry's bonnet and then up and away, along the large capping stones on top of the red brick wall. At the end of the wall he stopped by the tall sunflowers the children had planted in May. They had grown tall and strong with the sun and a good feed of 'smelly water' from time to time. The faded flower heads had dried and bent groundward, heavy with seeds fit to ripen in the sun.

Then Peawee was gone.

# Chapter Eleven

Harry was quite alone, not even a murmur. He hadn't expected to feel 'nothing'; that had never happened before. He had always thought of a story or a time gone by, or what Jake was doing in the garden, but today there was nothing. Then he tried to put himself in Peawee's place as a tiny wood fairy being ripped of his wings, the very brutality of it. Then to lose your father, home and identity – how much could anyone so young endure? It almost broke Harry in two.

Harry usually stood tall against his pole, proud of the garden, honest in his approach to each day, but now for the first time he just wanted to flop down in a heap on the ground. He took a moment to look around him and once more the piano music came flowing into his life. Above the melody the birds sang their tunes and the insects chatted, while the hens scraped here and there. This time the piano music stopped and restarted. A pause. Once more the piece started at the beginning and this time was completed. One of the children of the Pink House was having a piano lesson, little fingers trying to spread out over the notes in the right order in some form of time and expression. The visions Harry now had were of the children and they were the future. He took sustenance from seeing and hearing them explore everything, excited to turn over a simple stone and name the slimy slug or gleefully watch a tiny zebra spider dart about. He couldn't form a judgement or future without hearing the rest of Peawee's tale.

He remembered one morning Rose and her mother came to feed the hens. There was an old Marans hen they call the 'Old Buzzard' who could be temperamental at the best of times. That morning she was the last to emerge from the henhouse, making an odd sound and seemed in a grump. Dolly looked at her daughter.

"The old buzzard is in a sulk this morning, maybe she is broody," she said.

The little girl skipped about thinking this problem over, then looked at the hen and then up at her mother. "Give the old buzzard a lollipop and then she will stop sulking," she said.

Harry would love a lollipop – just maybe it would

stop his sulking. Something sweet, that was what he needed.

The sun was burning warm on Harry's face when he heard the gate open. Along the path came Mrs D and Dolly all dressed in their white bee suits. Something sweet! It was the honey harvest time, thought Harry. It was later this year, as Dolly had to recover her strength after giving birth to her daughter. The late July rains had set the scene perfectly, for the hot sun and dampness had produced the right humidity to let the lime nectar flow. The trees were buzzing with every winged insect in the district, or at least that was what it sounded like.

The barrow was full of all kinds of useful things covered with a large sheet. They stopped in front of the scarecrow. "Here we go, Harry," said Mrs D. "The poor bees, we are going to intrude upon them and take their hard-earned honey, so they will not be happy today. Don't worry, we won't take it all, we will leave them a honey 'super' on each hive for their winter food store."

Harry loved the way Mrs D talked to him about the progress in the garden.

Off the ladies went towards the orchard. Soon the smoke filled the air around the hives and they busied themselves taking the frames out and wiping the bees off them with a goose feather, before placing the frames into an empty box in a large black plastic bag. When it was full of frames it was tied up and on to the next one. One hive had three full honey supers, a good quantity for this far north of the country. It took a while, but soon the hives were reassembled and the wheelbarrow was loaded with frames of honey all covered up – no bees could get under that sheet to retrieve their honey.

The bees were now rather angry, as someone had taken their food stores. It was late into the year now, autumn was on its way and although the sun was shining the bees were not a happy bunch. The scarecrow wondered what life looked like from behind the dark veil, with all those thousands of bees whizzing by, intent on bombarding the wearer of this defensive garment. The sound alone would put most people off the art of beekeeping, so they are brave folk who don the white suit and venture to harvest the honey. In some lands these people are called 'honey hunters', which Harry took as the right word to use. The ladies seemed to display an air of calm as if worries were beyond them; they may well have been trembling just a little on the inside. Imagine what the bees were thinking!

The ladies made their retreat still wearing their bee suits and veils, to the dark shade of a large apple tree. The bees soon left them alone, returning to their hives, and the ladies emerged from under the branches and back through the garden. They simply couldn't wait any longer and stopped in front of Harry. In a quick flash of movement Mrs D and Dolly had lifted off the white sheet, flipped up their veils and taken a frame of honey out of the box. They looked at each other with enormous smiles on their faces and in unison plunged a finger deep into the wax-capped comb, twisting their fingers and digging into the honey before quickly popping it into their mouths. They murmured sheer contentment as the warm honey oozed around their lips. Then they quickly covered up the wheelbarrow and went on their way, giggling and still licking their lips.

"Oh, sorry, Harry!" said Dolly, and briefly returned, to put some of the golden honey onto Harry's lips before going on home to extract the delicious warm harvest.

As the two ladies approached the gate they stopped in amazement. There was no-one about at all; it was like a picture from the *Mary Celeste*. The washing had been abandoned, half hung out on the line and the rest either strewn on the ground or still in the basket. There was a trail of coloured pegs leading to the back door, while a rake had been left up against the fence and the mower abandoned, purring in the middle of the lawn. The ladies hastily pushed their barrow back to the house, to find the family safely inside with all the windows tightly shut. What was all the fuss? One or two of the bees had been angry and no-one was waiting around to find out if they would sting them or not. Later that evening they would extract the golden honey and there would be honey for tea.

Then Harry heard a shrill squawk. What a noise! Over in the orchard the mother hen and her brood of chicks were being harassed by the bees. The bees had diverted their attentions onto the chicks. Disaster was averted as the hen soon found a dark spot under a thick quince tree, where the bees didn't bother her. She lay down and the chicks buried themselves under her wings, all safe. The bees soon calmed down and returned to their hives, and the garden was at peace once more.

Harry's lips were now covered in warm honeycomb and the golden goo was trickling down his chin. Sticky little bits of wax clung to his lips. He could smell a hint of peppermint – or was it the aroma of lime tea? When his face started to tickle he noticed a couple of bees had landed on the honey. They started to gather it up into their guts and transport it back to their hives, to restore it into an empty wax cell, back to where it had come from. Harry remained very still, for he could feel the humming wings as their tongues came out to dip into the honey. Eventually all that remained of this stickiness were a few pieces of wax and they floated down to the ground. But for the first time in his life Harry had tasted the honey from the garden, and it was sweet.

Transitions can be a difficult period for anyone and through the year there are moments that headline these events. The honey harvest could be said to be the end of the year, but it is not. Although they leave some honey for the bees, there will still be a sugar feed needed to top them up for the winter, until spring is well on its way next year. Some local beekeepers even take their hives up the Angus glens to the heather for a late crop of a dark, deep-flavoured honey from the purple hills. There was still a lot of work to be done for the bees and their keepers, and Harry hoped he would remain outside for a long time yet.

Harry could now feel a real chill in the air these autumn nights. The colours in the horse chestnut trees and rowans were slowly changing and if a strong wind whipped up this night, they would start to fall by morning. Berries from the elder bush were ready for pressing and sweetened for their syrup. Heat this up with a sprig of thyme and it will keep winter colds and flu at bay. It was the favoured hot drink in the flask that Jake brought to the garden to drink while sitting on the cherry bench. Jake had been busy this past week and many of the beds were now empty of their crops and well-rotted dung or compost layered over them ready for the rotovator to churn it into the soil. There it would lie until the following spring, ready for the next rotation of seeds to be sown.

Empty beds, empty feelings. Lonely nights too, as Button-box had not returned. Where was his friend? Had he too been shattered by learning of Peawee's hurt? The scarecrow needn't have worried, as the black bird was circling above the garden before descending to Harry's side.

"*Craw-craw!* Now that was close! Someone actually tried to shoot me today, damned cheek. All I did was have an excursion up the hill. I am so glad there is a 'no-shoot' policy at the Pink House and farm. Sanctuary, at last. How was your day, Harry?"

Harry looked at his friend. "Trust you to bring some trivia to the end of the day."

"Getting your tail nearly blown off is no trivial

matter, I can assure you. I am most upset with your reaction to the matter, I don't know why I bothered to come back at all." The crow turned to go.

"Please stay, Button-box." Harry was ashamed at his nonsensical remark. This was not about him – or was it? "I just…" Harry's eyes closed as his words faded off.

Something was wrong and Button-box knew he had to stay. He hopped along Harry's arm, turned to his friend and with his soft wing wiped the scarecrow's tears away.

"We will never know what Peawee has been through," Harry said, "but I have tried to imagine the pain, the loneliness, the sheer trauma, and then try to be the best I can be."

"Harry, you are always the best you can be. You have the ability of uncritical acceptance, which is rare in the garden, and everyone admires that quality. Come on, tell me about your day."

The two friends ended the day embraced in each other's stories, but there was no delusion that Peawee had yet to finish his.

# Chapter Twelve

There was to be a rude awakening to Harry's sleep. An infernal racket was drowning out the peaceful and tranquil morning. It was not long before the culprits came into view: the ewes were being herded up the barley field. The crop was long past gathered and stored, which left the stubble to harden in the field and very little else growing. This was perfect for weaning the lambs off their mothers – the lambs were taken away to fresh pasture, while the ewes were put onto this stubble. Here the lack of good food would dry out their udders and prevent mastitis or ulcers forming. It looked harsh on the sheep, but once their milk had dried up they would be put onto lusher grass to get them fit for tupping in November.

However, the noise. What a noise! The lambs wanted their mothers, but by this time of year they were quite capable of surviving without the milk. It would take a few days, but they would soon settle to the new grass alone. Meanwhile, it was *baaaaa, baaaaa! Baaaaaaaaaaaa!* All morning long, *baaaaaaaaaaaa!*

It drowned out anything Harry had wanted to say or even think. Well into the night the sound of the lambs could be heard in the distance, until eventually all was quiet. Sometimes it was good to have straw in one's head, thought Harry, while Button-box tucked his head under a wing to sleep.

Within a few days the lambs had settled into their new routine. In the garden too a new routine had taken over, with designs starting to be drawn up. A huge bag of spring bulbs had arrived by post and everyone was mustered into helping, with the reward of a beautiful display on the bank down to the burn next year. They came to the vegetable garden later on in the day and dug random holes about the borders, where the children dropped three bulbs into each of these, covered them up and with a smart pat, job done!

"Best to do all that before the bad weather comes." It was Peawee. "It will look stupendous in the spring, don't you think, Harry?" Peawee had the habit of appearing, as if onto a stage, to deliver some kind of theatrical monologue. It was wonderful to see him.

Harry greeted him. "You look better, my friend."

"I took myself up into the forests, sat myself down and listened to your words. They worked on me and, when I heard the low melody of the stags' rutting on the hill, I remembered the words of the White Hart. So it is time to finish what I set out to tell you both."

The group of people had already gathered up their trowels and trugs and headed indoors for their well-earned tea. Jake was the last to leave, pausing briefly to look back over his patch with joy at a good day's work well done. Did he see Harry Also's bonnet move as if something was hiding underneath? Oh well, best leave it at that, thought Jake.

"Did he see me, Harry?" asked Peawee.

"Well, if he did it didn't worry him. Now where is that bird? Oh, there you are. What have you got in your bill?"

Button-box had momentarily sat on the red brick wall while the folk left the garden. His eyes sparkled as he flew down onto Harry's shoulder.

"Just some roadkill," said the crow, as he gulped down a small morsel of dead rabbit. "Now the nights are drawing in there are more animals caught in the vehicles' headlights and killed. All the more for me to eat – yummy!"

"Crows do a great job at keeping the roads tidy," said Peawee.

"Why, thank you, we have our uses," replied Button-box.

A cold breeze had started to whip up around the fields

down at the rosebay willow herb. The tall, handsome arrowheads of pink flowers, so good for late honey, had now given way to fine, delicate seeds and with one gush of the wind a mass of these floated up into the air. They swirled around, up and down, and then dispersing into the sky, like the fairies themselves dancing on the breeze, floating into space to another field or wayside.

Silence. No-one knew what to say, or who was to speak next, and it felt awkward to the three friends, but Peawee knew he had to continue.

"Every day she seems further from me and I miss her. I can only just remember her perfume, the essence of her," started Peawee. "I would wake to my mother crying and realise her sadness was bound up not only in the grief for me and my nightmare, but also in the loss of my father, her soulmate. They had been wee-fairy sweethearts. We were now adrift together living off my mother's wits. She bathed my wound and comforted my mind. She made me the dock-stem whistle and I learned some simple notes and tunes.

"Then one day we arrived in an enchanted landscape. It was so beautiful and the woodland was lush and green. The forest was filled with Wuidwisps and woodland fairies who made us welcome. My mother had become tired of flying away; this would be where we settled and made our home. But her guilt kept eating her up inside and she felt ashamed, blaming herself for what had happened. It made life simpler for her to tell the tale of fostering me, as a tiny Wuidwisp, from a forest on a remote island on the west coast. My imaginary parents had died and no-one was there to take me in, so she became my foster mother." Peawee opened out his hands and showed them to his friends. "You see, my father and mother were tree fairies, so at least my hands had the scaled skin to grip the bark of trees like the Wuidwisps. As my strength returned I simply pretended to be a Wuidwisp, learning from the others how to move so deftly through the forest. I never gave anything away as to why I wasn't as quick as the others; I just made them think I wasn't very clever around the trees. I would often fall but just got back up, again and again. We couldn't tell anyone I was really a fairy with no wings or the Droigs would've been after me. I had no-one to talk to, I felt so alone."

"Do you mean you never took off your jacket, not ever?" asked the crow.

"No, not in front of anyone but my mother. Fortunately the scars are very hard to see, as I was so young, but the scars in my mind are more difficult to mend. In all aspects of my life I was a Wuidwisp and yet I felt so alone. I had to keep pretending for my mother's sake and she for mine. That is how I came to be."

Harry was looking towards Handbag Wood as his very fibre seemed to tremble, but now was not the time to fall apart. "*Craw-craw!*" Button-box gave a whistle of amazement, which broke the silence, and Peawee was able to continue.

"Then one day I knew I had to make a journey by

myself. There was so much confusion in my head, as I felt anxious about the other Wuidwisps discovering the real me, yet I didn't even know the real me. I came upon Handbag Wood on my travels. It was a perfect place for someone in disguise and wanting a new start. So I stayed. There I am, said and done."

"How does it feel to be able to tell someone your real story? All those years of living with this knowledge?" asked Harry.

"I'm not sure. Do you believe me in all I have said and done, or do you feel deceived and – most importantly – will it alter our friendship? I would understand if you didn't trust me anymore." Peawee looked from Harry to Button-box and back again.

Harry looked at Button-box and the crow's eyes suggested a hint of impatience.

"Yeah, right!" said the crow sternly. "So you think we would just abandon you as a friend, just because you hide behind a disguise to, erm, shall we say, 'save your life'? You have got to be kidding me, Peawee. What kind of friends do you think we are?"

"Only the best," replied Peawee meekly.

"You daft wuidy fairy – or is it a fairy wisp? Best friends stick together."

The crow had said the right thing at the right moment, not too silly but a necessary relief from the high tension of this serious tale. Could Peawee move on from this? Only time would tell.

"Please don't tell anyone – as far as they are concerned

I am a Wuidwisp and I manage fine with that. I can survive anything, but not humiliation and rejection from the woodland folk of Handbag Wood. They have always been good to me."

There was a flash of wings. A fairy was about.

"Tell anyone what?" It was Peardrop up in the cypress tree.

Someone had to think hard, but it was Peawee who managed to think quickly.

"That, erm… I had decided to come to your celebrations for my foster mother's life, and for the new baby girl at the farm. I was being a little selfish drowning in my own misery and that is not fair on you guys. It is harvest festival time, the pumpkins are fat, the jams have set and there is honeydew wine. What more could we need?"

There was a long pause. Did Peardrop overhear the truth? The crow, Harry and Peawee waited anxiously in the silence. A fairy then floated down next to them and then another, and finally Peardrop appeared.

"Did you say honeydew wine?" asked one of the fairies.

"Yes, my friend, lots of it!" said Peawee. "The honey this year is dark and golden, as the bees feasted not only on the fine lime flowers, but the huge oak tree was sticky with honeydew this year. Millions of aphids were all over the leaves and their poo is very sweet."

"Party time!" cried Button-box. "With aphid poo?"

"Don't worry, the aphid poo is as sweet as nectar, so

the bees gather it up in their gut and turn it into the dark honey in their hives. The bees allow the fairies to take some and turn it into a scrummy drink."

"Party time indeed, and the party is coming to a garden near you," said Peardrop, pointing to Harry. Harry smiled; he was very relieved the atmosphere had changed. He looked at Peawee, who gave him a big smile, as if to say 'it will be OK now, don't worry'.

"When shall we come to the garden?" asked Peardrop.

"How about tomorrow night?" suggested Peawee.

"Tomorrow night it shall be – that will give the water fairies time to get here. Peawee, is there anything special you want to remember your foster mother by?" asked one of the fairies, who was busy looking under Harry's hat.

"I think she would be very happy with knowing we were all together in one fellowship in this beautiful garden. I will bake a quince cake, her favourite, and Peardrop, can you see if it is not too late in the year for fairy lights? Oh, and there will be music, lots of music." Peawee was on a mission and Harry was content to see him immersed in this undertaking. Colour had returned to his face and he was standing tall once more.

The fairies gathered themselves up and away, to invite all Peawee's friends and neighbours to the celebration. Everyone would be involved.

"This could be the very thing to help you start afresh, take that step," said Harry. "There is only one life: here in the now, there in the future and the one in between.

We will help you embrace it, feel your pain and your happiness along the way."

"At least it seems they didn't overhear my sad story and it is about time I accepted their invitation – they have all been so kind. I'll see you guys later then, I had better bake the cake." With that Peawee was on his way.

Harry looked at Button-box, who was snuggling down to sleep beside him. "Have you ever seen the Droigs?" he asked.

The crow yawned, his beak wide open. "No, only the mess they have left behind." He almost hissed through his nostrils. "What they can do to fairy folk is unimaginable." With that the two friends were asleep, exhausted and drained.

Darkness was deeper than usual, as if the very night had heard the tale of the Droigs. There were no owls hooting, or stars sparkling in the sky. It was cold and empty and near to a frost off the hills.

# Chapter Thirteen

Up with the lark! Not this morning. The cockerel was crowing over and over again. Somehow Dolly had sneaked past Harry and let the hens out without him waking. This was unheard of in the garden. The cock crowed again and a perfect echo sounded back from the woods. A still, clear night this time of year heralded a frosty start to the day.

"Morning, Harry! Why, I have never seen you asleep this late on such a lovely morning." The squeaky voice of Moleskin was at Harry's feet. "In fact, it is a little late for me to be above ground. I needed to smell if there had been a frost last night. I think autumn is here as leaves are on the ground."

"Yes, and the rest are inside out with colour," added Button-box, also a late riser this morning. "Look at the woods."

Autumn colour could come this quickly. Up in the glens there would be avenues of yellowing trees, while later the golds and reds would take over the hillside. If the wild winds came this glorious landscape would soon lie as a carpet on the ground, but for now it began a slow metamorphosis.

"Are you coming to the party this night, Moleskin?" asked Harry.

"Oh, yes indeed, Peardrop has been to everyone with the news. It will be a fine time for Peawee." With that the mole rushed away down his hole and out of sight, safe in the earth.

"It will be fine, won't it, Harry?" quizzed the crow.

"We can only hope it will be," replied Harry, just as a hoverfly pestered his nose. Harry went cross-eyed as he tried to focus on the little insect. It looked more like a bumblebee, with a camouflage of coloured stripes, but it wasn't furry. Others looked like wasps. Most of these insects were now gone, while the butterflies had fed well on the late flowering sedums and moved on to find places to hibernate in the woodshed or crevasses in trees and scrub. All were hoping for a mild winter this time.

Jake had arrived and Button-box took to the air. The gardener spent the day digging up the potatoes, leaving them on the ground to dry and harden the skins. Then he selected the best for his seed for the next year and the remainder were put into large paper bags, to store and eat over winter. The carrots and beetroot were clamped in dry sand and all that remained in the soil were the winter cabbage, leeks, sprouts, curly kale and the parsnips. Jake was always willing to try new varieties, so different plants would be seen each year. Unusual gourds were now ripening in the polytunnel. These would later be varnished and set neatly in a fine bowl as a central display come Christmas time. A large bonfire had rid the garden of the remaining trailing plants, such as the French and runner beans. Onions had been lifted and strung in plaits to hang up over winter, along with shallots and the garlic. It had been a fine year in the vegetable garden, so many things had been better than expected – even the sweetcorn was bountiful and sweet this year.

Jake was alone in the garden. There were no children this day to muddle his spirits or lighten his load, but he was content. They had all helped to put on a huge display for the harvest festival in the village. A wheelbarrow full of straw with a massive pumpkin had been the centrepiece and everyone had contributed what they could. There had been a ceilidh, music and laughter as an expression for thanks for the earth's bounty this year and for visions to the future crops of the land. His last job of the day was to fill the bird feeders with the mixed seeds and hang some fresh fat balls they had made on to the trees. These contained more seeds and fruit pieces, but it is the lambs' fat that helps build up the birds' reserves for winter survival. The netting over the fruit cages had long been removed after the harvest so possible snow wouldn't break it. As always the last remaining fruits on all the bushes were left for the birds. Even when the blackcurrants were pruned and the branches taken back to the Pink House for the children to pluck the fruit off the stems, a few of these were left behind to give fruit to furry or feathered foragers. That is when the fairy folk would come to the garden and gather goodies to take away and eat or store for the winter.

Yes, Jake was happy with his year. He had one last look around before heading home for his tea. He stopped at Harry's side, straightened the bonnet on top of the scarecrow's head, gave a big sigh and spoke quietly to him. "We've done well, Harry Also. I'll leave you here just a little longer until the frosts really come and brown the leaves away. I will be starting the cutting back soon, so you can keep me company until I've finished that job."

Jake was gone and Harry was alone once more. He didn't mind this, for he was looking forward to the events to come, as he hoped Peawee was too. Harry looked around, but the one thing he couldn't see was the sunset on Ben Lomond, for it was behind him, behind the high red brick wall. One day, he said to himself, he would leave the garden and then he would see new things, new visions beyond this horizon. Until then, he would gaze at the changing colours in this garden. The gentle winding-down and surrender to the darker seasons was on its way and most living things were taking full advantage of the prolonged amount of sunshine this year. Bees were feasting at every opportunity on flowers with late nectar like the ivy, privet, fuchsias, autumn crocus and the long row of Michaelmas daisies. Over fifty butterflies were canopied over the buddleia, as well as on the second flush of the wildflowers in the meadow. Many other insects dissected his vision; it was as if the vegetable garden was a resting station on a highway where visitors came to refuel. It was a frenzy at times as the nights came earlier.

Tonight! Of course, how could he forget the party? It all seemed very quiet and he hadn't heard anyone or seen Peawee and the other fairies. Surely Moleskin would be about soon. Maybe they had decided to have it up in Handbag Wood. It was unlike Harry to be impatient in thought, word or deed, but if he had nails he would be nibbling on them by now. Maybe he had the wrong night, maybe it was tomorrow night, as he couldn't remember exactly which side of midnight he had said 'tomorrow night' for the celebration. Oh my, he was getting into a state.

It began to rain. Harry felt that would seal the fate of the party: it would be postponed. Hold on, that wasn't rain he could feel on his cheeks! Something as soft as silk brushed past his face! It was raining, but it was raining rose petals. The fairies were here! Rose petals are as sacred to the fairies as the day is to the night. Reds, pinks, whites and apricot petals drifted everywhere around Harry. He felt a little ashamed of his concerns over the abandonment of the party, but now was not the time.

The air was faintness, soft and inaudible, but Harry knew something was coming. He could feel them. Then he saw the haze of light approaching from Handbag Wood; it started as a glow amongst the trees then moving like a gurgling stream down to…

"Hallo, Harry!" a fairy called out. They were here; they were everywhere. A whisper of fairies was upon the garden.

"Hallo, Harry, how's you?" asked one.

"Hallo, scarecrow. Party time in the garden," said another.

So many woodland fairies and their colours lit this evening's paradise. Harry's garden was alive. Many of the fairies' colours were changing, as the hawthorn, chestnut and ash trees' leaves turned away to autumn. Some were still in faint hews of gold and the yellows of late poppies clinging to the stones, which only fuelled the palette of this night. Their wings beat fast, as they collected and decorated the scene. Seed heads from the clematis, and spiralling inula fading yellow but feather-soft to the touch, made the perfect tabletops. The elder fairies then came with the feast and laid it on the floating tables.

Harry had never seen so many different foods. On each table was placed lavender bread, tiny acorn cups of nettle, mushroom and pine-cone broth. Lots of autumn salads foraged from the woods were decorated with pieces of borage and nasturtiums, and calendula petals were mixed in harebell bowls. The desserts were of blackberry, damson and dried peach skin crumble, covered in lemon custard. Harry could see sweet-chestnut biscuits, rose-petal jam, corn mash and much more, to add to this melange of salubriousness. That's a big word for a big feast, thought Harry.

"So where is the dance band?" asked Button-box, as he landed on the high wall above the proceedings. "Can't dance without music!"

"You have to be a little more patient, crow," called out one of the elders. "We are waiting on the crickets to provide the rhythm section, and for Peawee to attend."

"Let's hope he is coming," said Button-box, trying to be witty, but Peardrop was not amused.

"You should have been named Buffoon-box," the young fairy retaliated, upset at this remark from the crow.

Button-box had been put in his place and bent his head in shame, but not for long. He shook his cheeky self. "I can't seem to help myself with stupid comments at the wrong time. You're right: this is not the time or place for flippancy. You have all put on a fantastic display tonight. I will go and find Peawee – I expect he is more nervous than we are. Won't be long!" And away the crow flew.

Everyone had stopped what they were doing at Peardrop's comment, but the crow had only said what they were all thinking. To cap it all the water fairies and nymphs hadn't arrived. Maybe the journey was too dangerous. They would need to travel down the burn to the well, where the water came up from the rocks below and then across the fields. The whole evening could be a disaster if they didn't make it! The nymphs didn't like being away from water: it is their natural environment, and with no wings they would be vulnerable in the open ground.

Harry, true to himself, knew exactly what to say. "Shall we have a cup of tea while we are waiting? It won't be long before Peawee is with us. What have you brought us to drink? It smells wonderful!" Good old Harry.

"You could tell us one of your stories while we drink tea to start the party," said Violet.

"A short tale from the bush, then," said Harry, and he waited while the fairies gave everyone a cup of hot elderberry syrup or chamomile tea. "Last year Dolly was walking through the woods with the little girl when she heard a faint shrill coming from a small rhododendron bush. On closer inspection she could see a very young tawny owl, ever-hopeful that its pathetic cry would attract its parents, who could then continue to feed him on the ground. Curiosity had taken the better of him: as he'd looked out of the hole, high in the trees, he'd leant over just a little too far, and oops! He'd fallen to the soft ground below! Dolly knew the small bird, all fluffy and wide-eyed, would be vulnerable to the fox, and so commenced to look for its nest. After walking around looking for possible holes in trees she came to one candidate: a large horse chestnut tree loomed above. All around the base of the tree were small pellets of fur and bone and the remains of birds and mice. Bingo!

They were the very signs of owls feeding and raising their young.

"Dolly went back to the farm to fetch William and the ladder. He managed to balance the ladder very close to the hole and then held it steady, while Dolly aimed up it. First she tucked her jumper into her trousers and put the owlet down the front and ascended the ladder. She then had to undo her trousers, hoping they wouldn't fall down, so she could disentangle the bird's claws from the wool and extricate it from under the garment. She peered into the hole to see two sets of large eyes staring back. It was definitely the right nest, so she put the deserter onto the ledge, where it immediately popped down on top of its siblings. Just as Dolly was fastening her trousers to come down the ladder the small owl showed its face at the opening and gave her a little present."

"Was it a gift to say 'thank you'?" asked Peardrop.

"I'm not sure if it was to say 'thank you', but what arrived in Dolly's lap was the powder-puff cotton-tail of a pre-consumed rabbit, beautifully brought up in one cough. Dolly was so taken with childlike joy, she nearly wobbled off the ladder, to which William shouted up in his usual tones: "Don't fall off, you won't bounce like the owl!" They both laughed as they walked home. The little girl was enthralled by this adventure with a happy ending, and back in the tree a happy trio peered out."

There was much laughter. Harry was a master of timing and so too was Button-box, who appeared with Peawee moments later. He was followed by his Wuidwisp friends, all carrying quince cakes. The band arrived with whistles, bells and space drums made from bottle tops.

"Sorry, guys, we are late, so many cakes to bake. I hope they don't taste too much of bonfire cinders." Peawee then took up a stance on Harry's arm and called the gathering to order.

"I would like to thank everyone here in the loving memory of my foster mother and for the new life here at the farm. William and Dolly's new baby will have a very special place to grow in. I think …"

He was unable to finish his sentence for in the distance there came a new sound. Someone was humming, whirring sounds and bobbing sounds together with laughter. In the cover of the wildflower strips came a new vision, one filled with lights. Fairy lights!

"The water fairies and nymphs are here. Look over there!" said Harry.

It was a magical sight that continued to move towards them. The water fairies and lily nymphs had come together using their experiences to make garlands. The tiny individual flowers of the blue ceanothus had been preserved in a bubble of honeydew with a glow worm attached. These were then strung onto the spiders' gossamer threads. They were now hanging between the water fairies, and as they flew towards everyone a pathway of light emerged from the meadow. It was spectacular in its innocence. The evening was ablaze, as more and more fairy lights drifted over the assembly. The nymphs carried dried poppy heads, filled with smouldering herbs as scented lanterns, which were planted in the ground. The air was fragrant with the sweetened scents of hyssop, lemon balm, rosemary, woodruff and sandalwood. Angelica seed, elecampane root and coriander were all heating slowly to release their fragrance.

The nymphs had travelled upon the backs of some of the water fairies. The gang of fairy lights eventually came to rest in the trees, along the wall, between pruned bushes and all around Harry. He was surely in a dream. There was lots of giggling as the fairy folk welcomed each other with the trials and tribulations of organising a light show, food and dancing, and all in less time than a hiccup. It was to be worth every bit of energy used. It was the time of year to generate ideas of renewal, as nature dies down to rest, or even decline into death itself. A time to discover inner strengths and bonds and to say farewells.

It wasn't long before everyone had eaten their fill and Peawee was singing his songs and playing jigs for all to dance to.

"I can't remember a happier 'sad' time," said Moleskin, who had also arrived just in time to see the lights come to ground.

"You couldn't have said a truer word, young Moleskin, you seem wiser beyond your years," said Harry.

# Chapter Fourteen

All the friends of the garden were together and it seemed only like yesterday that the mole had been asking 'if spring had sprung'.

Even so, as this merry crowd continued in celebration, a dark mist was creeping up from the south over the hills from where the glow of the cities came. No-one seemed to notice the change of atmosphere and the chill drew in like a noose. It was with perfect timing that out of the darkness came the Droigs, hundreds of them catching up the nymphs, before they could flee. The others had now scattered, but they couldn't just leave their friends.

"Ha! That will teach you all!" a gruesome voice

echoed from the darkness of a shrub. "Now we are going to have some fun."

A large, smelly Droig entered the arena. He was pointing a long finger directly at the crowd, while his other hand gripped the top of his own head. A ramshackled smoke hung from his sticky lips. He was tall and skinny with grey puce skin, and his nose was squashed up his face like an open skull. His eyes lacked focus and he was all trouble.

His grotesque appearance sent the fairies up high into the sky, leaving only Harry to face the gathering of pure evil. There were simply too many Droigs gathering at the scene, and many a nymph was caught up struggling helplessly to free themselves from these monsters. Unable to fly like water and woodland fairies, the nymphs are very vulnerable, having left the sanctuary of their grottos and waterways. The fairies dashed about trying to help by picking them up onto their backs, but so many were now trapped.

The Wuidwisps were agile and escaped up high, only to look back at a dreadful sight.

"Come now, everyone, let's have some pied juice and life won't seem so bad."

The Droig placed a small bottle of yellowish liquid up to a nymph's lips and forced him to swallow the vile, sticky concoction. Within seconds the nymph collapsed to the ground, rolling his eyes and unable to focus on the enemy. The life was draining from his soul and he turned a pale grey, while gasping for a breath that wasn't there. He arched his back in excruciating pain. Soon all was still and no-one dared to move.

Harry broke the silence. "Now you have had your fun, you can go back to where you came from. Your kind of nastiness is unwanted here." Button-box had disappeared, no doubt to hide away.

"Oooh, look! A silly scarecrow!" replied the Droig. "What a shame there is nothing you can do, because you are just stuffed with straw. A useless piece of garden furniture!" He continued to bait Harry by pulling in another nymph to his side.

"What do you want, Droig? You never venture this far north out of the Fractions."

It was Osmunda, an Irish water fairy, as old as the hills and wise with them.

"We are here for fun, get it? Fun! Come on, join in!" The Droig was now circling round, looking up at the hovering groups of frightened fairies. By this time some of the other Droigs had given pied juice to their captured nymph and the earth had become a pitiless floor of misery, where once there had been joyful dancing.

"*Stop!* You must stop this slaughter!" Harry didn't know if he was angry or afraid, but he had to think quickly or all the nymphs would be lost, and then who would be next? "There must be something you want. We are peaceful folk."

"Well, now, Droigs, what a shame. No war, no putting out the fairy lights." Their leader circled round, grimacing at each face as he spat at it. He couldn't reach the fairies, but the horror did and their spirits were fading.

Osmunda flew to Aroid's side, another young water fairy from the grotto.

"Can we fight them?" she whispered.

"No chance, there are too many of them. I've never seen them here before because we don't like their juices – there must be another reason."

"Oh yes, water fairy, there is a reason for our happy entrance to your lovely festivities. We venture this far beyond the Fractions because we have come to collect one amongst your crowd of Wuidwisps, and until he gives himself up we will continue to give this delicious pied juice to the nymphs so you can watch them suffer. Don't worry, their trip to the deadlands is wonderful, all lights and psychedelic motions." The Droig was now licking his lips of thick saliva.

"There is no Wuidwisp you want here," intervened Harry.

"Yes, there is! One amongst you, shall I say an impostor, has lived with you as a lie." The Droig was really enjoying goading the quivering group, while his mob restlessly grunted nastiness.

"Who, tell us who?" Aroid was getting impatient with this creep's sense of humour.

"One of you Wuidwisps is in fact a woodland fairy with no wings, and his father killed mine in cold blood. If he doesn't give himself up we will destroy you all and your woodland community. He will die so you can all live and then we shall leave." He was now coughing into every word he uttered as he puffed on yet another ramsackled smoke, his nostrils burning with the acrid smoke. His eyes had lost focus, his mouth turned down and his skinny body was swaying. Once more he gripped his head to stop the tremor.

Harry became like stone. In sudden realisation he knew it was Peawee the Droig was talking of. His dearest friend had not found peace after all. How was he going to save him? He would have to think quickly. No time, no time in the now. He needed time; he needed the dawn to come, and come now.

Before Harry found an answer Peawee had come to rest on the cherry bench. "I am the Wuidwisp you seek. Now take me and leave the forest folk alone." There was a gasp from everyone in the garden.

"You! I have been hunting you all my life! If you are the one, then take off your jacket and show us the scars where my father ripped out your wings, and then we will leave," groaned the ugly, grappling monster.

The crowd gasped at this new knowledge. Peawee had been the one torn near to death who had hidden this from everyone in fear of his own life.

Peawee began by putting his precious dock-stem whistle in Harry's pocket. "Look after it for me, Harry. One day someone will play it again." Peawee stood up straight and unbuttoned the jacket slowly. With every button a tear fell from his eye. He knew he had failed his parents now. It was all over: his mother was now dead and he would soon join her and eat quince cake with rosehip sauce. He just wished he—

"*Come on!*" shouted the Droig. His impatience was showing, but Peawee kept his calm.

The jacket was open and he moved to ease it off his shoulders, when a loud cry came from the apple border. "I am the one you seek!" and a Wuidwisp joined Peawee on the cherry bench and began to take off their jacket. Then another came, she was very shy but gained amazing courage from what she had seen. Down onto the bench she came, unwrapping a shawl as she did so. "Take me, Droig, and then leave. Look, I have no wings anymore: the Droigs ripped them out of my back when I was very young." She was crying bitterly into her shawl. Peawee was at her side and wrapped his jacket around her shoulders.

There must have been seven or eight Wuidwisps now showing their scarred backs. This was unprecedented. Where had they all come from? Why had they not spoken up before?

"We will eat well tonight, my friends." The Droig laughed as he grabbed Peawee into his spidery arms.

"Harry!" cried Peawee. "Harry!"

But Harry couldn't see or do anything to save his dear friend.

# Part Four

# Winter

# Chapter Fifteen

Harry woke screaming from his nightmare. The Droigs had come and shattered everything good about the garden. They had ripped away Harry Also's lovely eyes, which now lay discarded on the ground, broken and lost. Harry had no visions to the present or future, perhaps a fitting punishment for his useless, straw-stuffed body – useless, as he could do nothing to help on that awful night. The fairies and nymphs had only come to the garden because Harry couldn't get to the grottos in Handbag Wood, where the nymphs would have been safe. No! They had to come to the garden because this useless lump of straw, Harry Also, was stuck in the ground unable to budge. Now the garden was empty of woodland folk, no fairies, no Wuidwisps, no nymphs and no fairy lights. All gone. Peawee was gone.

Another day came with all the cold of winter. The scarecrow's sense of sound and touch had only been enhanced with the loss of his eyes. The wind was bitter, the rain icy on his face, and he could smell the woodsmoke of bonfires and clearings. The sound of heavy boots on the gravel path had replaced summer sandals – a subtle difference, but one nonetheless. He had missed the fireworks and sights of Halloween, the carved pumpkins with a beeswax candle therein, glowing through the pretty or gruesome pictures cut into their sides. The children had come once more to the garden to collect the giant orange fruit and smaller neeps to cut their designs into, but none had noticed that Harry had no eyes – or if they had they didn't say. They always came as night fell on All Hallows' Eve (as it used to be called) and hang apples and oranges pierced with cloves along his arms to ward off the evil spirits. They placed dried fruit around his feet as food for the fairy folk and a garland of lavender around his bonnet.

For some reason it had all been forgotten this year. Harry's face was all forlorn.

The cherry bench was unoccupied more often than not, so stories were hard to come by in winter. At least he still had Button-box to cheer him up. Now where was that bird? It was the sound of another bird that caught his attention. The sound began to fill the early morning air. It was a strong beat of a large bird, wide as it was loud and louder it came on. Harry remembered this sound but couldn't put a picture to it. If only he could see! A memory started to drift by, a sound of the deepening winter or late spring. It was getting louder, deeper, louder as the beat drowned out the very air these birds were flying on, attentive, throbbing, a whistle of wind. These had to be large birds and lots of them with calls to keep them together, a call, an explosive, deep-toned *oonk*. They passed overhead and Harry remembered: they were swans, here to overwinter on Flanders Moss on the floodplain of the River Forth. Here they would graze all winter, keeping together in family groups looking more like flocks of sheep, as Harry had been told. He could now see them in his mind's eye, these huge, majestic white birds flying at great speed with long, outstretched necks. With their black webbed feet tucked neatly under their bodies they were streamlined in graceful perfection. Harry didn't understand why some birds came here for the summer and then left to travel thousands of miles away for winter, while others flew away for summer only to return and overwinter here. Why not just find somewhere to stay all year round? Maybe one day someone would come to the cherry bench and discuss the matter and then he could know.

"Those birds are so big, I could hide under their wings and get a lift to Iceland in the spring."

"You daft bird!" Harry was startled by the friendly crow.

"Yes, but just think of it. Hundreds of miles without any effort and you get to see a beautiful country, bathe in natural hot springs and eat loads of fish." Button-box was in good form. "Why not, I say."

"I would miss you," sighed Harry, all glum again.

"I would return a few months later with lots of new stories for you."

"That could be good." Harry twisted his head away from the crow.

"Now, don't do that, I have brought you something very special today. My mother didn't call me Button-box for nothing."

Harry could hear the sound, in fact, two sounds, like a double click on the cherry bench. Metallic, that was the word to describe it. "Are they what I think they could be?" There was anticipation in his voice and the swans were all but forgotten, as they disappeared over the woods.

"They could be," tormented the crow, but with a giggle in his voice. "Shall we see, so to speak? Excuse the pun." He was being his jovial self. Had he forgotten Harry's dilemma? Well, not altogether, how could he? They were both locked into this dreadful situation – except Harry's was terrifyingly personal. Button-box's only hope to help alleviate some of Harry's pain was lying on the bench.

"Crow," demanded Harry, "describe them to me: the colour, size, number of holes, what kind of buttons they are."

"*Craw-craw!* I get the message!" The crow now hopped along the bench and, taking up a button in his beak, hastened to Harry's shoulder. He let the object slide next to Harry's cheek. It was satin-smooth, like a mushroom skin.

"Colour, tell me the colour."

"They are each an eight-petal-pointed star-shaped beauty. There! Imagine that!"

"Oh, I am close to it. Continue."

"They are dome-shaped, sweeping slightly backwards, and each section is filled with enamelled colours of the rainbow, separated by a stencil of gold."

"Oh my! Rainbow eyes!" Harry was excited about his new eyes. His friend had been true to his word that night, when everything had gone badly wrong. He had promised to find Harry some new eyes and here they were. There was only one problem.

"How are we to attach them to my face?" Harry asked.

"I've been thinking about that and the orchard fairies are going to help. No worries, they are spinning the lambs' wool as we speak and will be along as soon as they have enough of the fine thread. Burdock is looking for a convenient thorn to hew into a needle and Archibald's your uncle."

"Don't you mean 'Bob's your uncle'?"

"Oh no, my uncle is called Archibald."

"When will they come?" Harry had forgotten his downcast demeanour and was now standing tall, in anticipation of an historical moment. Button-box, the cleverest of crows, had found Harry some eyes. He would see again into his beautiful garden.

The button felt good against his cheek and his imaginings were all over the place, with fusions of colour and light. He had learnt so much without eyes, travelling a different path to find answers. Now he was impatient for the fairies, with their Shetland wool thread, to come and sew on the buttons the crow had found.

"Where did you find them?" asked Harry, trying to fill in the time. "They sound like the most amazing buttons!"

"You know I have been collecting buttons since I was just out of the nest, hence my name. My mother would always call me Button-box, each time I came home with another bright round and usually shiny treasure. I knew they would come in useful one day. These two are my favourites and you will soon see why. Here comes Crispin from the orchard and they trail some yarn."

Harry decided to play it cool and calm. He couldn't believe the fairies were coming in the middle of the day to sew his new eyes on, but then there hadn't been many folk about recently. It was all pure fairy magic. As soon as the two fairies Crispin and Jasmine arrived, Button-box held the sparkling buttons up to Harry's face. The thorn needle was perfect and easy to thread the woollen yarn through the end. A deft dance around and the first eye was magically on Harry.

"Wonders of winter! I can see all to the very edge of

the orchard! The trees look so bare, it is as if I missed the fall."

"Now don't move, Harry," whispered Jasmine, "or you may get an eye on the end of your nose."

"OK, OK, but I am excited. It is like coming to the garden for the very first time. The last time I saw the…" But Harry couldn't say the rest of the sentence, as he remembered the horrors of his last visions.

"Don't fret, Harry," said Crispin, "and don't move." The two fairies sprinkled a little of their magic onto the pair of enamelled buttons and then flew off to fetch one last vital piece of the puzzle.

"What now?" asked the shaking scarecrow.

"Here we are," sang the fairies. "Here we are. Now you can see for yourself. Look!" and they placed a shard of looking glass in front of Harry.

Harry opened his eyes. Everyone looked at each other and then at Harry, who was leaning one way, then the other. As if spellbound, mesmerised by their beauty, Harry began to smile.

"Can you not see? Do they not work?" asked the crow.

Harry couldn't speak.

"Harry?"

Still nothing, but huge tears rolled down Harry's cheeks. He sniffed them away.

"I don't deserve such beautiful eyes," he said. "I am nothing but a useless old scarecrow who couldn't frighten a mouse."

As the tears came so did the fairies, the orchard fairies, some from the stables, the woods, and they all hovered around Harry. The last to arrive were the water fairies. Within moments Harry's world was filled with fairy dust sprinkling down on him and his shadow.

"Come on, Mr Harry Also, no need to snivel."

"OK, Button-box, I will stop. You are all so kind, I thank you from the bottom of my boots." Harry began to look all around him. His world did look different, wider, fuller or just new. It wasn't as he remembered. "I can't get those awful images out of my mind, but I think these eyes will help me. I am so sorry about the nymphs, but I never really understood what happened once the Droigs had taken my eyes. Button-box just keeps saying it will all be OK but it isn't OK: I need to know."

Poor Harry was getting quite upset with the memories. Someone had to explain why Peawee was gone. It was Osmunda who came forward and sat on Harry's shoulder, not far from the scarecrow's downcast face.

"I'll tell you, Harry. I will be honoured to do so; it was a night to fill any storyteller's mind."

# Chapter Sixteen

Harry relaxed for the first time and let the storyteller begin.

"I will start at the time when the Droigs took your eyes. Peawee and the others had stripped down to show their scars. No-one realised just how many fairies young and old had concealed their hurt, their scars, too afraid to come forward. Now there were a dozen brave ones on the bench. You were the first to react, Harry."

"Yes, I remember. I wanted to call out to the folk of the Pink House. I wanted to call out to anyone to come and end this struggle, but all I could do was shout in a kind of panic." No-one moved, all focused on their memory of that night. "*Stop!* I kept calling louder and louder, but no-one came and all the Droigs could do was laugh. They had Peawee."

"Yes, they had Peawee," said Jasmine, "and he wasn't afraid any longer to show himself as the fairy they had searched for. I have never seen anyone so strong in his mind. But I don't understand why they took your eyes, Harry."

"To literally shut him up," said Button-box. "But he kept on shouting for help, trying to drown out the horror of the Droigs. The gang's leader, called D-cay, signalled a small group to get Harry. They rushed at him, up his legs, and before anyone thought what they might do, the Droigs had ripped his eyes off and thrown them onto the ground, where they broke apart."

"All was darkness, just a kaleidoscope of noises I had never heard before," continued the scarecrow, now fully aware of these dastardly crimes. With his eyes restored he was able to follow the story as it was unfurling from his friend's lips. "Then Peawee stepped down from the cherry bench into the waiting D-cay, whose face was alive like a maggot feeding. He could hardly control his trembling hands as he stretched his arms closer to Peawee's brave body. No-one could move."

"OK, but when do we get to the good part?" whistled Button-box.

"Why don't you tell the next part then, old friend?" said Harry, knowing his friend was eager and only too willing to tell this tale.

"Are you sure? I mean, only if you insist, I can—"

"You tell us the end of the story," said Osmunda.

"I thought you had flown away that night out of fear for your own life," added Harry.

"You had no faith in me, Harry!"

"I just couldn't see any way out of the infernal mess, but you are right, I should have had more faith in my best friend. I am sorry, Button-box."

"Don't beat yourself up about it. Now here is the good bit." But poor Button-box still couldn't finish his story, as a little voice coming from amongst the carmine winter stems of the dogwood shrub now interrupted him. It was Moleskin, in a hurry not to miss the famous story.

"Wait for me!" he panted as he hurried along. "I can't miss the best bit!" He sneezed and settled down at Harry's feet. "You can carry on now. Thank you for waiting."

"OK, Moleskin, never too late for one more. *Craw-craw, craw-craw.* Well, one by one the crows of the Yellow Spot tribe landed on the top of the red brick wall. One by one we spread our great black wings and crowed. *Craw-craw.* It was a stunning sight of seven large black crows looking menacingly down on the crowd below.

That was when the Droigs showed the first signs of fear. They knew what crows are capable of. We are birds of the Fractions too. With our large beaks and sharp claws we are like vultures, seeking out the carrion with deadly accuracy. We can smell trouble and blood from a long way off."

"I can see you all now," said Osmunda. "You just sat there with your shiny chests all puffed out and your beaks hissing down on us."

"I wondered what that noise was," said Harry. "It made my straw shiver."

"We were impressive, weren't we? Oh yes! But then I saw D-cay grab Peawee and I knew there was no time to lose." Button-box was now dancing on the ground in a mock battle, hopping in and out, dodging ghostly Droigs. "We all took to the air, our legs poised under us and our sharp claws ready to spring open, as in one swoop we divebombed the unprepared Droigs. The sounds that came from our throats frightened even me, but it spurred us on into the fray. I was very frightened that we had left it all too late to save the nymphs, let alone Peawee."

"Your actions seemed to gel the fairy groups into action," said Crispin. "We took the fairy lights of honeydew and dropped them onto the Droigs. The sticky mess was everywhere as they tried to run through it, so they became rooted to the spot, unable to flee the crows' attack. With arms flailing above their heads they screamed a gruel of a sound."

"That was a brilliant idea from you guys – it gave us time to grab the Wuidwisp fairies and put them on the high wall," said Button-box.

"All except Peawee: he was clamped in D-cay's festering grip. I can smell him even now, that loathing mass of skin and bone," said another fairy.

Harry nodded; he could distinctly remember their smell and would never forget it – not even the compost heap or slurry spreading on the farm smelt as badly as the Droigs. He wondered if this was the smell of the Fractions.

The friends had not noticed that they had been joined by the Yellow Spot tribe, sat atop the red brick wall. Their place of honour, it seemed, from now on. There were the two youngsters from this year's nesting and they sat proudly between their families. True to their name they each had a yellow spot, one in a pure yellow tail feather while the other one was around the top of her beak. They all sat tall and nodded at Button-box to continue.

"D-cay managed to use the other Droigs as stepping stones over the honeydew drops and dragged Peawee away. He was crushing the life out of him. The crows picked up the screaming Droigs, three or four at a time like wriggling worms, and they carried them off in their beaks to be dropped from high into the raging Endrick Water at the bottom of the bank field. Some were even finished off in mid-air, as the crows pulled them apart between themselves and discarded the remains to be eaten by field or fowl on the ground. The crows could not get to D-cay, as he used Peawee like a shield each time they tried. Their beaks could easily have killed the Wuidwisp fairy, but no-one had imagined what would happen next."

"Oo, oo, come on, I love this bit," squirmed the mole. He was getting just a little excited.

The story was interrupted again, this time by the cats, PC and Lucy, out on a scavenge. All the fairies hovered just a little higher into the trees. The mole had run up Harry's trouser leg when he heard the cats on the gravel and was shaking the straw inside with his nervous jitters.

"It's OK," purred PC. "We'll not be hurting anyone in the garden, not even the mole. We have been listening to the tale – can we join you for the last chapter? Peawee was our friend too."

"Of course, PC. Delighted that you can join us. Come on out of there, Moleskin," said Harry, and the mole peeked out from the top of Harry's waistband.

"I'll stay right here for the ending."

Everyone returned to their places and settled down for the climax. Button-box looked at all his family and friends. He was proud to be part of this garden. He cleared his throat.

"We were losing," he said. "I was losing a best friend. Peawee's life, the life he had fought so hard for, was being taken from him, from us. In the confusion and mass of wings and screaming Droigs I could see one chance and only one to get at D-cay. I had to be deadly accurate, or my beak would kill Peawee and not D-cay. I launched myself from the wall with only one target in mind. I don't know how, but the hysteria of the mob seemed to part like a tunnel. As my speed increased so the hole opened up. I was now only centimetres from the ground and I could see D-cay turn and his eyes hiss at me. He held Peawee's body up to protect himself, but I had a plan. I knew he would protect his head using Peawee like an umbrella, and this would leave his belly exposed. I now flipped over, flying upside-down, and in one instant pierced D-cay and ruptured his guts. He dropped Peawee's limp body. I looped around and was about to collect Peawee, when D-cay grabbed him once more. His hand went down hard against Peawee's face to suffocate him."

Button-box's heart was racing now. Emotions he had suppressed until now raged inside.

"I didn't know I had a deeper strength, but with all of you doing your best that night I simply couldn't let D-cay win. There had to be a way to say no to the Droigs. D-cay was finished, but he was not taking our friend with him to the Deadlands. D-cay's entrails were spilling out onto the ground, yet he was still alive. The smell was overwhelming, but to us crows it is a delicious one. I stood over him and drew my wings around them."

"I remember," said Peardrop. "Everyone had stopped to see you encircle the two bodies into darkness with your powerful wings. It was all over. Dead Droigs everywhere, and the rest had run away into the shadows. The silence was only dulled by the panting of those of us still alive. What a panic!"

"Yes!" interrupted Osmunda with glee. "I can feel it now. I can see the scene now: your beak was covered in a mixture of blood and grime. What were you thinking just then, Button-box?"

"My only thought was for Peawee. In that last moment, had I killed my true friend, or had I got the Droig? I still wasn't sure."

"Harry?"

"Yes, Osmunda."

"Can you imagine the scene now?"

"Oh yes, I can see Button-box now. Please carry on."

The crow shook his head from side to side as if to dispel the memory. He was reordering his mind. It was no triumph, no moment of glory, no incredible deed. It was one moment in time that decided the fate of a friend, of all the friends of the garden and woodland here about.

"I slowly opened my fan-like wings. I couldn't bear to look, but when I did D-cay was nothing more than bits and pieces of Droig on the ground mixing into the gravel."

"And Peawee was..." But Peardrop didn't finish his sentence, as Osmunda told the crow to finish the tale. It was, after all, his story to tell.

"*Craw-craw!*" the rest of the crows cried. "*Craw-craw!*" they insisted, and so Button-box told the final chapter of the evening.

"I had my deathly claws wrapped around what remained of D-cay and Peawee. I could feel them, I could smell them, but I was afraid to look down – my head was pointing to the sky. I wanted to fly away. It seemed the world had stood still and I was the only one breathing. I had to face the truth. I had to see what I had done. I slowly, very slowly, looked down at the ground. One claw was squeezed tightly over the pieces of Droig, and in the other…" He paused a moment to regain his control. "Peawee was lying there under my claw, my foot protecting him like a cage. He was alive. I held him, caressed him. He was breathing there in my wings and he had survived. We had survived." Button-box fell silent with his memories.

There had been no cheering from the audience that painful night, no applause, no chatter of happiness. Many nymphs had died, but many more fairy folk had survived. As for Peawee? No-one had seen him since Button-box had lifted his claw to reveal a bedraggled Wuidwisp fairy. Peawee had stood up and everyone had cheered, then everyone had danced about like an eruptive fever in a frenzy of relief. He had simply turned, climbed Harry's trousers, retrieved his dock-stem whistle, hugged both Harry then Button-box and left. Not a word had been needed. The crowd had become silent as they watched him wisp away up into the trees, up and away towards the bright lights to the south, following the shadows of what remained of the Droigs.

"Come back, Peawee!" one of the Wuidwisps had shouted.

Byrony, the Wuidwisp fairy who had come to Peawee's side to reveal that she too had no wings, once more alighted onto the cherry bench. "You have to let him go. You have to let us find out who we really are now the secret is out. It is a whole new dimension for us. We need to know where we fit in. You will all look on us now as different folk, hurt, maybe, or even reject us because you can't cope with your own feelings of horror or guilt."

"That isn't true," Osmunda had said, as she realised that Byrony was right. "We could never dismiss what has happened to you guys. We will work together here, as a community, and go forward together." Some of them here in the garden couldn't or wouldn't understand what had occurred over the last few seconds of that awful night.

Harry now looked at his crow friend, then all around to the garden and beyond. The hills had gained a shallow white blanket. No-one had noticed the thin snow clouds in the distance turning the sky a whiter shade of rose pink. They didn't look menacing enough for a deeper snowfall, but winter was truly here and still he was upright in the garden. Where was everyone from the Pink House?

Harry's new eyes had brought him clarity. "We have to move on, embrace our friends once more and prepare for the new beginnings. Peawee has inspired us."

"What about your conquering hero, don't I get a medal or something?" said Button-box enthusiastically.

There was a stunned silence.

"Here is your medal, crow!" cried a fairy, as he threw a gooey lump of mud at the crow. Then the other crows did the same, showering Button-box from above.

"Mud fight!" called out a Wuidwisp. Soon there were tiny droplets of mud everywhere; Button-box was covered.

"OK, I get the point, you can stop now, guys," mumbled the crow, ducking between mud shots.

"Well, you did ask for that one, my feathered friend," said Harry, trying very hard not to laugh.

What a mess! A mud-encased crow was not a pretty sight.

"I still haven't learnt to keep my big beak shut," said Button-box, trying to shake off the mud from his body.

A breeze came through the garden and down the path to chill the air. Soon the folk were on their way with murmurs of farewell and hope for the future. Moleskin came down from Harry's waistband as soon as the cats had left and looked up at Button-box.

"You're still Button-box, and don't go changing too much or we won't recognise you. Now get yourself a bath before the night sets in." Away the mole scampered to the warmth of his tunnels.

The buzzard's high, shrill call echoed above them, so the Yellow Spot tribe encircled Button-box and escorted him away to clean up in their favourite puddles. He would soon be back to his usual self.

"*Craw-craw.* Good night, all!" was the parting cry.

Harry alone once more, Harry here and motionless. He gazed up at a nebula of stars before the clouds closed in and the snowflakes fell.

# Chapter Seventeen

In the morning Harry found his nose had a good layer of snow all the way along it. His arms were covered too and his bonnet felt very heavy. It had snowed far more than anyone had expected. Some late colour in the tall elecampane had all gone and the snow lay on the end of the very tall stems. The seed heads were being heartily stripped by the finches, pulling individual seeds up and out, briskly moving on to the next old flower head. They were very defensive of their castle-like food bin. Flashes of colour whizzed by Harry as the different finches baited each other for the best seeds.

The borders were left wild until early spring for the

wildlife, when Jake and Mrs D would cut back the old rotting growth, put compost between the plants and wait for the first bulbs to show. Always careful, they would split the overgrown ones, or dig out impostors, or generally redesign some areas to give a new blend into the garden. Harry's garden would be the tidiest patch, with all the beds covered in well-rotted manure or compost, and some would even be dug over by the end of the year.

Not this year. Where was Jake? Dolly appeared to feed the hens that morning, her large footprints in the snow filing past Harry. No 'good mornings', no cheer? A few moments later she returned. The hens, reluctant to exit their warm house, stood at the entrance tasting the snowflakes before stepping back into the shed. One or two ventured out, lifting each foot high up in front before gingerly putting it down in the cold snow. Then they ran for the cover of the trees where the snow had not yet settled and commenced scratching about for grubs. The usual *cock-a-doodle-do* escaped from Arcadia, the cockerel, who eventually emerged to look for his hens.

Dolly stopped at the iron gate. She put down her feed bucket and egg basket and returned to Harry. She reached over and ran her gloved finger along his nose to dispel the snow. It fluttered to the ground. Dolly stared at the scarecrow. Harry Also stared back. Something was wrong.

"Dear Harry, we seem to have forgotten you in all our worry. We must get you inside or you will rot. Poor Jake has had a stroke and is in hospital. It seems there is no time for the garden just now. Maybe once the snow has gone we can catch up a little. I must go and feed the sheep and take the rams out of the fields. The ewes should all be in lamb by now. I can't seem to think of lambing time in the deep winter, but the sheep need plenty of that wonderful hay with this snow on the ground. We must also do something about you, Harry, and we will." Dolly left.

Do something about Harry? What about Jake? What was a stroke? Harry was confused.

Dolly had the hay out in the fields moments later, helped by her little daughter. The sheep were all kinds of colours and the mixed bunch of Jacobs and Shetland sheep stood out brilliantly against the snow. The Suffolk rams had been taken away from the Jacob ewes in one field, while different colours of Shetland rams would remain a while longer with their ewes as their mating season ran later to the end of the year. Each colour-type ram had about a dozen ewes of the same colour markings. Katmoget, Moorit and two Emsket ewes were bred for their micro-soft wool, and nesting birds would pluck it from their backs come spring to line their nests with it. The fairies loved this super-soft wool and gathered tiny morsels of it for their homes and to spin, weave or knit the yarn. The colours made perfect camouflage for their clothing. If they needed bright colours they simply produced naturally dyed wools from the white strands within a fleece.

Rose ran over to the fence near Harry. "Oh dear, Harry Also, you are all alone. I will come and cheer you up." She ran off towards the Pink House. Moments later she returned with the other children, all neatly dressed in their woolly hats, gloves and wellie boots. The elder boy organised the group and they started to build a snowman, there beside Harry. It grew and grew until it was almost as tall as the scarecrow. They rolled one large snowball and placed it on the top of the body.

"You have a friend now, Harry," said Rose, and the children each donated a piece of clothing to dress the snowman. Potato eyes, an orange segment mouth and a carrot nose were the finishing touches to complete their masterpiece. The children were exhausted by the time they had completed their snowman and drifted back to the Pink House for a mug of hot chocolate. However, Rose remained and stared up at Harry.

"I must find some flowers for Jake. He is in hospital and isn't very well at all. I want to cheer him up." She looked around the garden, but there was very little she could find to bunch into a posy for Jake. She cleared the snow away and sat on the cherry bench and began to cry, only little tears but tears nonetheless.

Harry wanted to hug her and then he had an idea. He saw the crow and motioned for him to come down. Button-box quietly floated down onto the red brick wall behind Harry.

"What's up?" he whispered.

"Find some winter fairies fast, this little girl needs their help."

No more questions. The crow did as he was asked

and seconds later returned with Slim, Molly and Hazel. Harry told them the problem, the fairies huddled together for a moment and then flew off. At a signal from Harry, Button-box cried out *craw-craw! craw-craw!* and Rose looked up.

She couldn't help but notice the crow as he flew off the wall and over to a bush. The bush was shimmering with fairy dust, so the girl jumped down off the bench and went over to the bush. The pyracantha was laden with bright orange berries which the birds had not all eaten. The little girl knew she mustn't eat these berries as they were poisonous, so she just looked at them. The bush shimmered again and this time two sprigs of the bush landed on the ground, and they were so colourful that Rose didn't hesitate to pick them up. Another bush was shaking up along the wall, the winter marjoram in the herb garden. Another sprig lay on the ground and this time it was the aroma that the girl noticed. She picked it up, hugged the aroma and added it to the branches in her hand. There was another shimmer from another type of bush and another sprig for her posy, until her hand was full of winter magic.

Dolly came to fetch her daughter. "You must be cold, my lovely. Come on, let's go and get warm, then we can go and visit Jake."

"Look what the fairies gave me to give to Jake," and the little girl held out the winter posy.

"That is so beautiful," replied Dolly. "What a lovely idea, Jake will love it."

Pointing to a couple of bare twigs, Dolly added, "That was very clever of the fairies, for that is Chinese witch hazel. It has a delicious, spicy scent when it is brought indoors this time of year. The twigs will flower with spidery yellow blossoms. Well done in finding them."

Holding hands in the warmth of each other's company, Dolly took her daughter back home. Click went the iron gate.

"Thank you all!" cried Harry. "That was wonderful magic. Perfect, don't you think, Button-box?"

"Oh yes. Did you see her face when the fairy dust was sprinkled over each bush? What a picture."

The three fairies giggled as they waved their goodbyes. They too would have to get back to the warmth of their homes as it had begun to snow again. It soon covered the footprints made that morning and softened the sounds on the breeze.

Harry loved his new eyes; there was a brilliance about them, a sparkle even. He had never been left out in the snow before, but now he understood why he had been this year. Poor Jake, thought Harry, I hope he will be home soon, then he can walk in the garden and feel better. Gardens can be an oasis of healing, a place to rest or paint pictures, draw or sing.

More movement, thought Harry. Well, this is a busy place today, now what? The iron gate swung open and slammed against the fencepost and almost bounced straight back into place. If it hadn't been for the eldest boy from the Pink House quickly catching it before it did so, it may well have broken. He had a claw hammer in one hand and a pair of scissors in the other. This did not look good.

Hamish clomped along in his oversized boots and stopped beside the scarecrow.

With no word of warning he grabbed the pole and took off Harry's jacket. Then he cut the string on the two hands that held them to the wood, prised away the large nail holding the two poles together, eased the pole from along Harry's sleeves and Harry fell in a giant heap on to the ground. Be careful what you ask for, thought Harry. "*Craw-craw, craw-craw.* Not very dignified, but it worked." Harry heard the crow sing – or was he laughing those words?

The boy wrapped all of Harry up in a bundle but had forgotten one thing. Still on top of the pole was Harry's head!

"Charming, just charming," moaned Harry, as the boy took the rest of him to the largest greenhouse. He did, however, return to gently, this time, untwist the scarecrow's head.

"Sorry, Harry," he said, "it's all in a bit of a hurry. I have my homework still to finish. I'll put you right later." With that he left Harry's head lying beside his body on the dry ground in the greenhouse.

Harry could only see straight up to the roof of this glasshouse. However, the air smelt sweetly of herbs and dried flowers. This was where the lavender had been laid out to dry after harvest. Later it had been taken into the Pink House and used for all sorts of things. Calendula, rosemary, sage and many others were used in the kitchen, as well as some soaked in almond or grape oil to be used in massage therapy. Remnants of these plants were now scattered all around Harry and he bathed in their essence. Never mind his bedraggled state now; he was floating, intoxicated and alive with the aromas of the summer and the earth. Wow, it was good.

Harry was normally put away for the winter in the potting shed, but this was much more fun. He could just see the garden through the windows, in all its winter glory, while he remained dry inside. After a while the crow hopped into view and stood where a pane of glass had lost a corner, just beside the door.

"That's right, lying down on the job. Where am I supposed to roost with you like that?"

"I have no idea."

Another scurry of tiny paws and Moleskin appeared. "Welcome to ground level, Harry. You look kind of jumbled up and all in a heap," said the mole.

"Any more useful comments by anyone on my demeanour? I must admit, one gets a completely different outlook on the world from down here, Moleskin. I also think someone is making her winter nest inside my trousers and it tickles. Any chance one of you could have a look for the culprit instead of making silly comments? Thank you kindly." Harry was trying not to giggle at his predicament, but now Button-box was walking all over him, prodding and shaking his clothes. A squeak, and then another, as out of Harry's legs came not one but two very small shrews with twitching, long, pointed noses.

"OK, OK, we get the message, but it would have been a perfect location for the winter," said one of the shrews.

Harry apologised but assured them they would be better off in the woods away from the cats.

"Yes," said the other shrew, "but we think we have left it too late, as we can't get through the snow on the ground outside."

"Maybe we could come to some arrangement, if only I was a little more upright," said Harry. "Now let me see. Button-box, is there anything here I could use to help the situation? A box or something?"

"There is a deckchair lying on the ground at the other end, but apart from that there is nothing else," said the crow.

"Hopeless," said Harry. "I'll just have to lie here and gaze at the stars unless someone has a bright idea."

Someone almost came up with an idea and then it was lost in a flash. The pause was filled with a sudden rousing burst of song from a gathering of the garden birds. It was an explosion of trills and song bites. They were everywhere. Through the singing came a familiar voice.

"I have an idea!"

# Chapter Eighteen

Harry could only look upwards. The snow had not clung to the glass roof and he could see straight through, up at Peawee sitting on the very apex of the roof. There was someone with him, someone Harry had never seen before. A fairy.

Button-box flew up in a loop-de-loop, in all his excitement to be at Peawee's side. "Hi, and welcome to the winter residence of Harry Also. Come on down!" The crow was hopping up and down, then pretending to be on a tightrope walking all along the rooftop while wobbling from side to side, all in jest at the arrival of Peawee.

Peawee giggled at the artful buffoonery of his crow

friend, then turned to his fairy companion and said, "I told you he was mad!"

The fairy gave a shy chuckle. "Let's go down so I can introduce you all to my new friend. I have been away from this garden for much too long."

Button-box grinned his best-ever smile. "Jump on my back and I will give you a lift down. I only hope you do have a good idea for Harry's predicament – I am not sure he will last the rest of winter in a heap on the ground."

Peawee popped onto the crow's back, making sure he gave him a long hug, and down they floated while the fairy flew alongside them. A quick look around to make sure there was no-one around, and in they went through the lost pane in the door. Harry couldn't move his head; it was jammed with eyes straight upward. He longed to see Peawee – he had missed and worried about him every day since he'd left.

Peawee leaned over and smiled into the scarecrow's face. "Hallo, Harry Also."

A tiny face came out from behind Peawee. "Hallo, Harry Also," she said.

"Hallo, you two," said Harry. "Goodness, what a day."

"Yes, but it isn't over yet. We will be back in a flutter of a butterfly's wing." They were gone before Harry or the crow could call them back.

"Who was that and where have they gone now?" asked Moleskin.

Before anyone had time to respond there came a whirl of activity from the woods. A giant whisper of fairies and Wuidwisps arrived, pouring through the door and into the greenhouse. They hovered over and around Harry, and before anyone could say anything they were gone, as quickly as they had arrived. Peawee remained long enough to reassure Harry.

"Won't be long," he said. The shrews scurried about and came to rest in one of the corners, just a little timid with all the turmoil of the evening. There was barely time to think before the fairies returned, and this time with a long piece of rope. There was much laughter as Peawee directed the operations. First they tied the rope to the top section of the deckchair at both ends to make a large loop, like a handle. "OK, everyone, now lift it up slowly," said Peawee. Slowly and evenly the deckchair began to rise off the floor, and as it did so, the rest of the frame and fabric seem to fall gently into the right order. "Hold it there," shouted Peawee, "I just have to ease the frame into the notches as you gently lower it. Now!" The deckchair descended into the perfect position. It had a bright green frame and a bold red and white-striped cover, with a huge, yellow sunflower appliqued on the top.

"You next, Harry," continued Peawee, and the fairies tied the rope around Harry's shoulders before he could complain. Again it formed a handle and again they slowly lifted their friend. However, this time they didn't get very far, as the scarecrow was much heavier than the deckchair. They put him back down.

"Oh dear, we will have to find another way to lift you, Harry," said Moleskin.

Harry remained motionless. There was no real reason to worry. One by one the Yellow Spot tribe landed on the glasshouse roof, tapped on the glass and then entered. "Need some help?" said Sam, one of the largest crows you will ever see. He had an imposing yellow spot on his chest like a medallion. All the crows grabbed a piece of the rope and then with the fairies rose very slowly into the air. The slack was taken up, and then the real effort pulled Harry first up onto his knees, and then upright. They carried him over and sat him down in the deckchair. He flopped to one side but was soon straightened up. Now for his head.

"Gently now," said Peawee, who was coaxing the group. They got the rope around the head and lifted it in one go onto the neck of the shoulders of the scarecrow.

Harry was once more together. Wobbly, but together.

"I can see the world!" Harry declared. "I can see forever! Thank you, thank you, thank you, one and all! This is tremendous. You are so clever, Peawee. New eyes, new quarters and a chair to sit in. It feels amazing not to have to stand with my arms permanently stretched wide. I can see the straw in my hands and just relax them in my lap. I can honestly say, it feels great."

"Anything for an old friend," said Peawee, and everyone joined in the clamour of thanks and welcomes.

"Look, Harry, you have morphed into a scarechair!"

"But I don't scare chairs away," replied Harry.

"You don't scare crows either," said the crow, and they all laughed.

"In all this excitement you still haven't introduced us to your new friend, Peawee," said Button-box, whose curiosity was very obvious as he hadn't left her alone for a moment.

"I was just coming to that. She is a very special soul. May I introduce you to—"

"My name is Gentiana," said the fairy.

Peawee held out his hand. Gentiana took it and sat next to him on Harry's lap. There was much gossiping and chatter amongst the woodland folk, all eager to meet with Peawee's new friend. She seemed a rare soul, delicate in appearance with the bluest eyes they had ever seen. Her hair was of roughly braided locks, spiralling down from the crown of her head. Small shimmers of coloured lights were intertwined with the hair. Her wings were green and silver, matching the colours of her dress laying close down at her side.

"Welcome to the garden, Gentiana, and the greenhouse," said Harry, looking all about his new abode. "I don't know what is more lovely, you or my new winter home." There was a murmur and all the woodland fairies and Wuidwisps said their farewells. The night was closing in and a storm was brewing; they needed to hurry back to the protection of Handbag Wood. There would be plenty of time for Peawee's stories of his travels. In an instant they were gone, flowing away through the opening in the door like water through a spout, followed by the Yellow Spot tribe.

"Are you staying, Peawee?" asked Button-box.

"Are you wanting rid of me already?" Peawee laughed.

"*Craw-craw!* No, no, most definitely no!" replied the crow. "You couldn't be a prettier sight, except for your friend Gentiana, of course."

A little voice from the corner interrupted the group. "May we join you and make our nest now, Harry?" It was the two shrews, half-forgotten in their hidey-hole. "You did say if you were upright you could think of a solution to our dilemma."

"Yes, yes, of course. Come on up one of the trouser legs just to the ankle and settle there."

The shrews didn't need another invitation: they were off over the ground as fast as they could scurry and up the trouser leg. They munched and tossed around for a few seconds and settled in nicely.

"Thanks, Harry," came a muffled voice.

"My pleasure," replied Harry, only too happy to help. Button-box had found his usual roost on Harry's shoulder and settled to it. "It seems we are all together once more. Friends. This time, however, we have a new member, and it is lovely to meet you. How did that happen, Peawee?"

"We didn't think we would see you after that terrible night, you looked so lost and angry. What happened to you?" Button-box was always direct in his questioning. "You don't have to tell us if the pain is too much."

"No, it is alright, you need to know. I need to tell you things that brought me home – and home to stay – as a better Wuidwisp fairy. Gentiana knows everything that happened prior to our meeting, and I mean everything."

There was a sudden blast of wind from outside and large raindrops started to fall on the glass roof. They splashed onto the glass as they grew larger and louder. Then came a deluge of water as the rain intensified and the wind gathered speed. It didn't take long for a full winter storm to descend onto the garden. The snow was soon washed away and the darkness left the group of friends all huddled together, under the protection of Harry. Even Moleskin was tucked up neatly under a pile of the dry remnants of pumpkin plant – he had scuffled the soil up into a heap to keep warm and was not going to miss this story.

With a massive crash and thud the earth shook from under them. It seemed the very roof of the glasshouse would blow off. Then what? thought Harry. They had all just got back together only to be blown apart. He could only hope the greenhouse was strong enough.

# Chapter Nineteen

"Come on, Peawee, tell us your story, it will keep our minds off the storm," said the scarecrow.

Peawee looked at his new companion. She nodded and smiled at him in a melting moment of warmth and love.

"That night of the Droigs I had to get away, to follow these awful creatures of the Fractions. I had to do something, but I didn't know what. So, I followed their horrible trail of grime and despair, for they were a miserable lot, believe me. Many were badly wounded and died as they fell, while a few crawled and walked back the long journey to the city."

"Were you not afraid?" asked Moleskin. "No-one from here has been to the Fractions before."

"I didn't think about fear, Moleskin, I just had to see for myself. Anyway, I had been exposed, humiliated, and many nymphs had lost their lives because of me, so you see, I had to get away. There had to be some form of peace for me; I just couldn't go on the way I was doing as I was hurting the very folk who I loved. I needed answers and this was the only way I thought I would get them."

"You were very brave to go," butted in the crow. "You could have just stayed here."

"No way could I do that. I had to take a step up and get on with the life I have."

"So what then?"

"The glow of the city lights became more intense, as did my anxiety. I don't know what it was, but I just kept following the Droigs. The woodlands began to peter out and only the verges remained with adequate greenery to travel by. Then all along the roads there were huge lamps of glowing orange lights; the verges disappeared but there were small gardens in front of brick houses. Massive vehicles travelled the roads. Somehow this was the environment the Droigs festered in and seemed at home. Rubbish blowing in the wind, slimy gutters along the roadside, smells I had never detected before. I slept by day and moved by night, exhausted and afraid but determined to follow them all the way, to where, I didn't know yet."

"The city isn't all bad, you know," said Gentiana. "Against the odds there is good to be found in the Fractions."

"But not in the Droigs," replied Button-box.

"That can never be," said Peawee. "They found their hideouts and disappeared. But then I found something else."

"Was it Gentiana?" asked Moleskin.

"No, not yet. I followed the lights deeper into the city. There, amongst the high-rise buildings, stations, trucks and trains, I came across the most beautiful glasshouse I have ever seen. Like a sparkling, crystal cave it rises out of the ground, a mass of clear glass and light. I was spellbound. I found a way into this paradise and felt the earth breathe beneath my feet. It was warm and dry, and filled with plants I had never seen before. Different sections grew different plants, from large banana trees to delicate succulents in an arid section. Water flowed down over stepped falls to ponds with giant lily pads floating on them. Tropical houses dripped with warm water, and ferns and orchids grew up high in mossy trees. Greens I had never ever seen, sights to fill the senses and imagination. Oh, the wonders of this place you cannot imagine."

"Where were you?"

"He was in the botanical gardens, where we met," said Gentiana, all bubbly now with joy at the memory of that night.

"Yes," said Peawee. "I was so happy to find this amazing place that I settled down, took out my dock-stem whistle and started to play. The tunes came easily to me; they spoke in melodies I hadn't played before and

I felt alive. Then, from out of the trees and plants came Wuidwisps and fairies in unimaginable colours. They were exotic and beautiful. Their wings glowed and their hands carved out pictures in the air. I couldn't stop the music, as more and more fairy folk came down to join me. Then, out of one tall green stem with blue-capped flowers, came a young fairy. She drifted to the patch right in front of me and started to dance, seemingly unaware of anyone else until her dance became pure movement, almost devoid of the music. I was mesmerised by her dance. I played on and on, and the fairy folk cheered, leaving food and sweets I had never tasted before. The air was alive as I began to overcome my fears. I had started to learn about myself through this music and I saw a tenacity for life here in the Fractions and the very heart of the city."

A calm seemed to have settled on the group of friends after hearing the tale. "But you didn't come home straight away, so what did you do then?" asked the crow.

"The day came and fairy folk drifted away into their homes. Only one remained and it was Gentiana by my side. She was exhausted but still wanted to dance." Gentiana moved forward and spoke. "I wanted Peawee to keep playing and I to dance, as it made everyone so happy. He has magic in his music that heals a path and brings folk together, building bridges within a community. As the music changed to a jazz rhythm my movement became abstract, nothing complex, only awkward and angular. My body flung out in many directions, in small, repetitive routines, and then suddenly I would revert to a folk dance as I absorbed the softer music once more. I was alive to his playing, like a revolution in my soul. I couldn't leave him."

Peawee continued their story. "We stayed together and travelled around, playing, dancing and telling stories of our adventures to anyone who would listen. We met other fairies tortured by the Droigs who had survived, helped by their friends and community. We met others too afraid to talk about their hurt until that moment. Now they would be believed. We shared our stories. My mother would have been happy with all of this. Our music and dance brought a sort of solace to folk. We were asked to visit the sick and dying, to bring some happiness to them. I just couldn't believe what was happening. I had been so ignorant of the good in folk and yet they tolerated me and then accepted me. We went all over the city and with Gentiana it was a magical experience; she was the perfect guide. She was the inspiration I needed to stop imprisoning myself in doubt."

"Why did you not confront the Droigs before they disappeared?"

"That is a good question, Button-box," said Harry, who was quietly taking in the occasion. He wanted to know why Peawee had returned.

"The atrocity of that night long ago and here in the garden had festered in me in all those days of travelling to the city," explained Peawee. "When I got to the

Fractions I realised there is a demarcation line between good and evil, and I was not going to enter their way of living by taking revenge. I said 'no' to the Droigs and let them slink away. Better for knowing where they had come from, I did not want to be part of their misery any longer."

There was a murmur of agreement and admiration amongst the gathering that Peawee had indeed not taken out his anger on the Droigs. Harry smiled one of his smiles.

"We could end with a tune and a dance," said Peawee. Before anyone could say anything Peawee took out his whistle and was playing a jig that no-one in the garden had heard before. Gentiana slowly got up and alighted on the soft ground beside Harry. As if in a trance she glided forward and began to dance. As she swirled into the routine her skirt became full with colour and sparkled like jewels. It flowed outwards until the dance took her into the air. The music and motion became one. The audience stared in admiration with eyes wide open and only the sound of the lone whistle could be heard over the wind. As the storm intensified outside, so the music and dancer captured the evening, until there was no more energy and their bodies stopped, breathless and still. "That was beautiful, Gentiana, it was as if you showed us your very soul," said Harry.

There came a loud roar from the wind and everyone jumped into being, but no-one seemed afraid.

"But you have not told us the real ending to your

story, and why you came back." Moleskin was very alert and didn't like unfinished business.

"That is true, but there isn't much else to say. I had to come back. I had to come back to the garden and all of you who had always been here for me. I had to show you that I had found a way to be myself. Yes, I could do that anywhere, but there is nowhere like a garden." Peawee looked at Harry. "And there is no-one like Harry Also." Everyone smiled heartily at the two young fairy folk. They were content in each other's life. Gentiana had made the decision to follow Peawee wherever it took them, and for now it was here.

# Chapter Twenty

In the morning the friends awoke to a calm, with not a breath of wind or a drop of rain. The snow had departed and large puddles lay in the pathways. The henhouse was still standing and Arcadia heralded the morning light. Dolly came round and stared into the greenhouse, her breath pausing on the cold glass. What had she seen? A big beam of a smile ran across her face and she was gone. Harry beamed back from his deckchair!

Later on the sound of chainsaws could be heard around the woods and the friends learnt that a big Douglas fir had come down in the gale. A huge rotten hole ran all the way up the trunk and it had been too weak to withstand the storm. They were also mourning the loss of a number of good trees and the maiming of others only fit for firewood. There were floods in areas that had never flooded before; roads were a mess, a tangle of twisted branches and wood. It was the evergreen trees that suffered the most, as one of the cypress firs at the entrance to the garden displayed only too vividly – it had crashed down across the entrance and Dolly had to go around through the field to get to the chickens. She had only come into the garden to dig some horseradish root. "Quickly!" called Harry to all the sleepers. "Get up and away or the people will see you!" Moleskin rushed underground, Button-box was off to see if he was needed and Peawee took Gentiana off to explore his homescape.

"We will be back soon," and they were gone.

The day was long and no-one came back. No Button-box, no Peawee or Gentiana, and the shrews had left in a hurry too. He hoped they had made it to the woodland in safety. Some men had come and chainsawed the cypress tree into rounds and cleared the branches to the bonfire site. The iron gate was in one piece and so the garden was open again.

It was late in the afternoon when a group did come to the vegetable garden, a group that Harry recognised. Through the glass windows Harry could make out Mrs D, surrounded by the children of the Pink House, Dolly and one other person. He was walking with a slight limp and one arm was loose at his side, not moving with any usual rhythm. He was all wrapped up in a big scarf and a long woollen coat, and was slowly making his way towards the greenhouse. First they stopped and filled the bird feeders and laid dried fruit and fat balls on the bird tables. Bacon rind and old bits of scone and cake looked very appealing and nutritious alongside the rest. The man now seemed familiar. The little girl rushed to open the greenhouse door. It slid along its track and clinked to a stop.

Harry was now looking straight at the gentleman and he knew. How could he forget that endearing face? It was Jake. As the scarf fell away the man looked up and said, "Someone is sitting in my chair. He looks wonderful, well done, lad." Hamish didn't like to say that he had no idea how Harry had found his way into the deckchair. "You will make a fine apprentice here in the garden. I am looking forward to coming back to work and teaching you all I know. You will be the next generation who takes on the care of the land here and I feel pleased. We will get on just fine, won't we?"

Everyone agreed with Jake.

"Now where are those floating herb candles to celebrate our new beginnings?" asked Mrs D. "But don't put them too close to Harry, we don't want him to catch fire." Harry was a little perturbed by this statement. Fire, he thought, was not his favourite element, but he did like the candescent light from a candle.

The children each took hold of a candle. The small night lights were made from herbal wax instead of beeswax. The leaves of bog-myrtle and pale berries of the bayberry were boiled and the wax extracted by skimming it off the top and straining it. The candles were tiny, but once lit and floating in a saucer of water, they glowed and burned with a mild spiciness that filled the greenhouse with the aromas. They wouldn't last long, but their scent would last all through the night. There was a cheer; everyone had weathered the storm and their own personal battles.

"Well done, Harry," said Jake. "You made it through the storm. See you in the spring when I have regained my strength and you have rested… in *my* chair."

"OK, Hamish let's get the vegetables for tonight," said Mrs D, "to accompany the rib-roast beef from the farm. Rose and I have made a chocolate cake for dessert."

"With a marzipan scarecrow on top," Rose hastily added.

"Is there some of that excellent extra-strong horseradish sauce you always make, Dolly, to accompany the beef?"

"Naturally there is, Jake, I dug the root this morning," said Dolly.

"Did you remember to add a governmental warning on the lid? 'Beware! Makes your toes curl,'" asked Mrs D.

"Of course there is, and it does exactly what it says on the jar," replied Dolly. There was a festive mood in the air, but for now Jake would have to rest before the dinner tonight. He slowly walked home with everyone laughing, skipping and splashing about in the puddles as they made their ways home. Little Rose could always find something new to see or do in the garden; even the tiniest of differences showed up in her eyes, the eyes of the next generation of gardeners. She paused to pick a handful of snowdrops, just peeking through the damp soil in the garden – a hint of times to come.

Harry smiled to himself and thought it a shame no-one was here to see that. Or was there? A tap on the glass roof and Harry looked up. The whole gang was sitting on top staring down at the scarecrow. Tap tap.

In they came, all buzzing. "Jake is home, Peawee is home, everything is good in the garden."

"Yes, Moleskin, and soon spring will have sprung once more," said Peawee.

"Oh yes, and you won't forget to tell me this time, will you, Peawee?"

"No, my dear friend, I won't. I will be here for that occasion. You see, I found out one thing about this place that made me want to come back. I want to be remembered for the good in me, not the evil beside me."

"You have grown, Peawee: you took that first courageous step and found some answers, flourished and hurtled back to us. It has been a rollercoaster ride. You have brought Gentiana to be with us and she will blossom too. I could take another hour to digest the reasons why the people that live here give the garden such a peaceful atmosphere, but then it is still here when most people are gone." Harry paused, and then added, "Maybe they leave something."

The reunited friends spent many a happy time with their music, dance, songs and storytelling in the greenhouse until one day…

Spring had sprung and Harry Also was back upright in the garden helping Jake.

The End.

"It can't be the end."
"Why not?"
"Your tales never end, Harry."
"Good night, Button-box."
"Good night, Harry Also."

# Acknowledgements

Throughout my life I have had the privilege to travel and meet some amazing children and their folk. From one horrific moment in the life of a young child came hope and the trilogy 'The Tales of Harry Also'; this is the first book. I would like to thank my publishers Jeremy Thompson and the team at The Book Guild Ltd. for making this project a reality. The lovely Miriam Brent (42 Management and Production) gave me wise advice and encouragement; for my wonderful readers: Jo Ripley, Liz Lawrence, Eugenie Furniss, Jackie Ferrari, Sharon Vanderschuit (CAN), Elisabeth Chevalley (CH) and Heather Thompson (AUS) my thanks for all their ideas. Season's flower drawings are by Annie Minnaar, Lorna Baxter (Scottish artist) gave me confidence in my illustrations and Douglas Payne is my computer guru! School life can be daunting for any child living with Dyslexia but two of my teachers, Sister Mary Martina and Richard Brent, taught me (respectively) to champion the imagination of the storyteller and the use of the English language to fulfil my dream of being a writer/artist. My late husband, John Minnaar, didn't always understand the words I seemed to have invented on the page but his patience, love and skill gave me the final MS. I have known many strong, caring women who inspire me like my late Mum, Swiss Granny and Caroline Jean Cuthbert. But from my daughters Annie and Jessica I draw the greatest joy and self-belief; thankyou my lovelies. Thank you all, love from Celia.

More information at
www.celianormansmith.co.uk

*Ref: the woodcut illustrations*

"I love them. You make them so descriptive with such simplicity
and make just the right amount of space speak."
*Lorna Baxter (Scottish artist)*